Praise for

Hanna

"The journey is mesmerizing, heartbreaking and extraordinary—as well as beautifully told."

—Jenna Zark
Award-Winning Author of *The Beat on Ruby's Street*, and Playwright

"Readers will both cheer and wring their hands. . . . Jeger is blessed to be part of Hanna's legacy."

—Rona Simmons
Author of *The Other Veterans of World War II* and *A Gathering of Men*

"Told in a vivid and sober language, Hanna is a powerful personal narrative . . ."

—Iddo Moed
Deputy Head of African Affairs at the Israeli Ministry of Foreign Affairs

"Hanna is a riveting tale . . . a heartfelt and impressive tribute to the author's great-grandmother."

—Margaret Schuette
Editor of the Memoir *Journey Between Two Worlds*, by Karola M. Schuette

"Deeply moving . . . Hanna's story of perseverance continues to be relevant today."

—Stefanie Naumann
Co-Author of *How Languages Saved Me: A Polish Story of Survival*

"Both her writing style, and the strong dialogue in the book evidence the multifaceted skill of the author . . . This is a war story that is definitely worth telling."

—Ariëlla Kornmehl
Award-Winning Dutch Author of *De vlindermaand, De familie Goldwasser* and *Een stille moeder*

"It's a story of endurance that stayed with me long after I finished reading."

—Sonee Singh
Author of Award-Winning Poetry Book *Embody*

Hanna

By Magali Jeger

© Copyright 2022 Magali Jeger

ISBN 978-1-64663-757-7

Published by

köehlerbooks™

3705 Shore Drive
Virginia Beach, VA 23455
800−435−4811
www.koehlerbooks.com

Hanna

MAGALI JEGER

VIRGINIA BEACH
CAPE CHARLES

SPRING, 1941

"HANNA, YOU ARE COMPLETELY and utterly insane. I don't want to hear another word about this!"

These were the last words Ab said to me before slamming the door and storming out of our flat. My brother rarely called me by my first name, as people close to me usually used my nickname, Hansje, instead.

During our quarrel, my husband, Nico, had been hiding in the kitchen. He reappeared when Ab left as the noise of the slamming door must have woken up all of our neighbours during their Sunday lie in. Ab was my younger brother, though he couldn't help fathering me around.

"Again?" Nico asked uncomfortably.

"I don't care what he says."

The thing Ab and I had been fighting about was simply put: I wanted to have a child and he thought I was ludicrous for even considering it. We had been fighting for months on end, and every time I would bring it up, Ab sure had something to say. I assumed he didn't understand the necessity of wanting something more, someone of my own.

"Hansje, maybe it would be worth listening to what Ab has to say." Nico had a point. I always shut my brother down when he tried to intervene or make accusations. But there was something Nico didn't know yet.

"I was supposed to bleed two weeks ago."

His eyes widened.

"You mean—"

"I think I'm pregnant."

All of Nico's doubt seemed to disappear, and he embraced me. Nico and I had been wanting to have a baby for such a long time, regardless of what others around us were thinking.

"Have you told Ab?" Nico asked.

"The flat won't be small enough."

"Well, passion definitely runs in the family."

I lay my hands on my stomach. "That passion is carrying your little one."

Not only Ab, but most people thought I was crazy to want to have a child in these strange times. On a weekly basis, the waiting room of our family doctor would be full of Jewish women, and we all knew why they were there. Their morbid expressions revealed their intentions. These women, whether they were married or not, would receive pills in order to get rid of anything that could be growing inside of them. I admired them for their courage, as I was sure it must have been difficult. Most of them were desperately ready to start a family, though fear dominated their minds. But that being said, I couldn't be happier.

Two hours later, Ab came back home with our father, Mozes.

When they entered the flat, I noticed how much skinnier and paler father had become these past few months.

"Are you going to tell them the news?" Nico asked quietly. "No, I need to be certain first."

Father kissed my forehead. "Darling, how was tennis?"

"Ab bailed on me."

He gave me a dirty look but wasn't going to tell father about our fight. Father had other more important things on his mind. The last few years had been tough for the family. And now that mother had passed away, it seemed as though father's inner happiness was slowly diminishing.

I always tried to keep a smile on my face. Sure, I would've preferred to be able to live with my newlywed husband without having to share a flat with my brother and father. Though times were tough and there were sacrifices to be made.

Ab, Mozes, and Nico were discussing sports. They weren't allowed to attend the professional games anymore but still spent hours talking about them. I said that I would quickly go out to fetch a newspaper as the men wanted to read how Ajax was doing.

"Who are they to take away our radios, these bloody Germans," Ab said angrily as he lit up a cigarette. I hated it when Ab smoked inside the house.

I went downstairs and came across Klaas and Doortje, a couple that lived on the first floor of our apartment building. When our family first moved in, we had tried to befriend them and often invited the couple to have dinner at our place. They always gladly accepted, but never returned the favour.

"My condolences," Doortje said, and she kept her distance. "We wanted to come to the funeral but were too late to hear about it!"

"It's always difficult to lose a parent. We wish you all the best," Klaas said.

I replied respectfully, "Thank you. I'll give your good wishes to my father. He probably needs them more than I do."

Keep calm, I told myself. Klaas and Doortje had known about my mother's death since the day it happened. The apartment wasn't very big and everyone in the building had been talking about it. People knew her. They had seen my mother, Johanna, become more and more ill. Until she eventually wasn't around anymore. And then it was my father who, still in great health, started to look frailer. Our neighbours gossiped that my mother's disease might have been contagious, and they were scared that it might spread to others in the building.

Cancer is not contagious.

Doortje smiled. "You've always been a strong positive-minded one." Out of the corner of my eye, I saw Bonneka Leysen, our downstair neighbour. She crossed our path and said, "Well, look who we have here!" I thanked Doortje and Klaas again, trying to shake them off, happy to see Bonneka.

"The whole family is upstairs. Why don't you come up to say hello?" We went up to the flat.

"I see our newspaper has arrived," Ab said sarcastically.

"Nice to see the jolly bunch all together!" Bonneka was also a friend of ours and spent a lot of time at our flat. Her husband, Nol Leysen, was a captain at sea and was often away from home.

"Would you like some *boterkoek*[1]?" I presented her a small round cake pan and Bonneka took a generous piece.

"*Prosím!*" she said in Czech, and I knew it meant please.

"I managed to scrape together enough sugar and butter to get the crispy edge just right."

"You're a sweetheart." Bonneka hungrily gulped it down.

"Would you like more?"

---

1 **Boterkoek (or "Butter Cake")** is a traditional Dutch flat cake that contains mostly butter and flour. The cake is usually made in a special, round, butter cake pan.

"I shouldn't, but thank you darling! It's refreshing to experience some generosity. Not like all those Dutch women, who open their cookie jars to guests for a single bite and then hide them back in the cupboard."

Because of Bonneka's Czech origins, she strongly disliked how stingy the Dutch were.

"How's the baby fever going?" she asked. We often talked about my desire to have a child of my own, and she had been encouraging me to go for it. Ab was shaking his head disapprovingly.

"Hansje, wait a couple of years until things improve," father said.

"Wait for what? A bigger home, more food on the table? There is nothing else I want right now. Time is not going backwards. I'm twenty-eight, goddammit!"

"Your brother and I discussed it and—"

"That's very rich, discussing my uterus without me."

Father gave me a harsh look. Ab had spoken to father before I'd even gotten the chance to show him my point of view. It upset me how Ab felt he had the right to do this. I couldn't hold back tears.

"Hansje, stop arguing like a little girl," Ab interfered.

"Don't you dare patronise me!"

"Someone has to tell you the truth, and I don't see your husband doing it any time soon."

Ab looked down at his feet, realising he had gone slightly too far. I wiped away my tears and looked my brother straight in the eyes.

"It's too late now anyway."

All three men sharply turned their heads towards me. Nico was trying to gesture that I shouldn't have said anything. Even when Ab was condescending, he still managed to stay calm, unlike me.

"Oh, Hanna, congratulations!" Bonneka said, trying to brighten up the mood, though I wasn't sure whether she sounded excited or terrified.

"You're bluffing," Ab tried to keep his temper.

"You're pregnant?" father asked, "How long have you known?"

"Since yesterday."

"You can't possibly know. You don't even have a belly yet."

"Pish posh, Ab, it doesn't work like that," Bonneka intervened. Ab didn't know much about the female cycle. And it was true that I couldn't be certain until certain symptoms started to show, though I felt in my gut that it had to be true.

"A Jewish woman pregnant under German occupation, I would love to see how that turns out!" Ab was laughing.

"My child will grow up with more love and care than you've got in your left ass cheek!"

"Mind your words, Hanna Coronel!" Father used my maiden name when he was angry. He didn't like it when I spoke improperly or unladylike. Nico, who had been trying to stay out of the conversation, slowly intervened. "We aren't sure Hans is pregnant yet. Mr. Coronel, if it puts you at ease, we will wait a little longer until all of this endangerment dies down."

"We're not even allowed to enter local pubs anymore! It's been getting progressively worse boy. Nothing will die down."

I realised I had created a stir, which hadn't been my intention. The most important thing was for my family to understand where I was coming from. It was so difficult to explain what I was feeling and how badly I wanted a child. But it wasn't just me. Nico and I had spent many hours discussing our future and the dangers our decisions could bring. We both wanted the same thing, and to us, it wasn't a question of if—rather, a question of when.

"Hansje, I love you, but I can't see you put yourself into more danger, let alone another child's life," Ab said. It calmed me down. Even though I knew, deep in my heart, that my brother cared about me, his bluntness often felt inconsiderate and selfish. And it hurt me when Ab would have a go about me, as if I was incapable of making my own decisions.

"I know, but this is something I should decide for myself."

"Did you see the soldiers march this morning? With their trumpets and flags, they're pretending it's a victory. I even saw at least a dozen women giving out sweets to these so-called hero soldiers, as if they're the ones who deserve it!" Ab seemed a bit more enraged now. "They can shove their *Führer*-greeting up their arse!"

"Things aren't like they used to be twenty years ago."

Father often bitterly recalled a time when things had been easier. When the family still had their fortune and when he was a big shot diamond worker. We lived in a big house and mother threw lavish parties and gatherings. We had never been a pretentious or societally traditional family, but we enjoyed the freedom that money could give us.

Even when we had to move to the tiny flat, I tried to keep a high spirit. Ab and I had to leave school to go work and provide for the family. Ab said that my constant positivity would one day be my downfall, but I disagreed. Even though I appreciated my brother's bluntness, I always had my own ideals.

And this meant that I was sure of one thing. Soon, I was going to have a baby. Though, I realised that Ab and father would only see the negative side of it. Which is why I gave up trying to convince them or even mentioning it. From now on, I would no longer bring up the topic of having a child when my father or brother were around. Still, that didn't make me think about it any less. And nine months later, Betty was born.

WINTER, EARLY 1942

SHE WAS BORN on 15 January, five days after we heard the news that work camps for Jews were being set up in the east and north of the country. Things had changed in Amsterdam. During my pregnancy, I hadn't stopped working, as we were in desperate need of money. But I knew that once my little wonder would arrive, I'd immediately quit my job and spend all my time taking care of the baby. Every time I looked down at my belly, it was as if all of the negativity surrounding me vanished. Nico and I cherished the wonder growing inside of me. Which was also why every time someone even mentioned the word *abortion*, we immediately closed our ears, only thinking of the good moments that were yet to come.

For my father, things were getting even more difficult. He was in Apeldoornse Bos, a Jewish psychiatric institution, where he spent his days mentally bitter and physically weak. Mother's death was still a dreadful incident and questions kept roaming in his head. Father had lost his *joie de vivre*, which Ab found especially difficult. Therefore, he had stopped visiting him, as it was hard to see his childhood hero bedbound in that sort of environment. And when I was nine months pregnant, Ab didn't seem too joyful either. Deep in his heart, he loved me very much, and I was sure he probably felt a slight admiration for what I was going through. But this was something he would never admit, of course.

Ab and I were both at the office. He leaned over my desk, looking at my pregnant belly.

"Have you finally decided to take some time off work? Or are you going into labour in your office chair," Ab said ironically. He took a big puff of his cigarette. I forced a smile.

"Father wrote you something."

I showed him a sealed letter. Ab put it in his pocket. "I'll read it later."

"He's ill, you should go visit him."

"That man drains the life out of me."

"He's your father, Ab. What does the letter say?"

"I'll read it later."

I gave him a disapproving look. He took the letter out of his pocket and irritably ripped it open. The letter was shorter than the ones he usually sent to me. I analysed Ab's face, trying to understand what father could have written to him. He put out his cigarette, scrunched up the letter, and threw it in the bin.

"I'll go visit him," he said whilst putting back on his coat and exiting the office. When he was out of sight, I sneakily hunched to get the letter out of the bin.

Jan 10, 1942
Dear Ab,

For a whole week, I have been yearning at the thought of seeing you, but I have realised that you need some time away from me. I look forward to your visit, but do not want to rush you.

You should know that I am able to walk again. Unfortunately, my foot is still swollen, and the doctor concluded that I will soon have to be bedbound again to rest . . . it's no fun. I just hope to recover quickly. I've been writing to your sister, Hansje, and I hope she'll make sure that you read this too.

Why haven't you sent me the writing materials yet? I have been waiting for so long. Hansje sent me some paper last week, and I bought a pad with ten envelopes but had to pay almost a guilder for it. Because the people here will not give out a sheet or an envelope, they are afraid that they themselves will be without it . . .

I felt guilty and stopped reading the letter. How could I convince Ab to go visit father, before it was too late? The thought made me shed a tear, which I quickly wiped away. I looked at my stomach and felt a surge of joy.

Five days later, I was finally holding her. The little girl who Nico and I had been waiting for. She was wrapped in a cream-coloured blanket. We stared at her in disbelief.

"Our Betty," Nico softly touched her little hand whilst I was cradling her. Betty's eyes were closed, and she looked peaceful and innocent. She had my warm olive skin tone and Nico's defined facial features.

"Not a worry in the world," I said, observing my little one.

A few months after Betty was born, I took her to the Jewish cemetery in Ouderkerk, a village outside of Amsterdam.

"This is Grandma Johanna," I said to Betty, who was sound asleep. "You have never met her, and to my sorrow, she will never meet you. But once you get older, I'll make sure to tell you all about her and the amazing things she has done."

A curtain of clouds started to form in the sky, and I decided to leave before it would start raining. When we were on the train on the way back, it started to pour. We got out and I rushed home trying to protect Betty from the rain. She didn't seem to mind, as she was happily smiling. I got into the flat, soaked, and Betty was completely dry. I put her back in her crib when I heard a knock on the door.

"The door is open," I shouted.

Bonneka entered the flat.

"*Prosím*, sweetheart. Are you alone?" She had dark circles under her eyes. "Nico is at work."

Bonneka seemed relieved and walked over to Betty's crib. "You can call me auntie Bonneka," she said, smiling at the baby. Her voice was shaking a little.

"Not heard from Nol in a while?"

She shook her head. "You know how it is at sea," she brushed over the topic. "Suppose you have been too busy to keep up with the news."

Bonneka often talked about the things happening in her home country. "I haven't heard much. Things have been very quiet. However, I do remember some whispers about a German general in Bohemia creating a stir! What's his name . . . Heydrich!"

"Not that—"

Her concern scared me.

She took a deep breath whilst staring at Betty and moved away from the crib.

"The Jewish council have been sending people away."

"Where to?" I asked, and she shrugged her shoulders. "If it were just the two of you, then I wouldn't be so worried. Nico is a clever man, and you know how to stand up for yourself. And I can't imagine someone wanting to be cruel to such kind souls."

"Nothing will happen to us. I can promise you that."

"But now that you have a child—"

We simultaneously looked at Betty's crib.

"No one is going to harm a child," I said lovingly.

Bonneka didn't seem convinced.

———————

The next day, my close friend Pien and I went for a walk. Nico was at work and Bonneka was looking after Betty.

"We should take the kids to Scheveningen," I said enthusiastically.

Pien laughed. "Hansje, don't be ridiculous."

"I'm serious! Betty has never been close to sea, and it would do your Evi a lot of good."

Pien's daughter, Evi, had been a flower girl at my wedding. Everyone wanted to have Evi at their wedding. She was a pearl to look at, though it meant that she often took all the attention away from the bride.

"They won't allow us to go near the beach," Pien said.

"No one will say a thing! Remember those kids who were guzzling beers in the park the other day? They definitely weren't older than sixteen, and no one is stopping them. The law is filled with suggestive arguments."

"You know that no one will tell on a few Dutch kids for underage drinking, but our case is different."

"Then we'll go to The Hague. We're still allowed there, aren't we?" It sounded like a rhetorical question, though I wasn't actually sure if this was true.

Pien stopped and placed both her arms on my shoulders. "I don't know what I would do without you and your good spirit," she said, and I instinctively hugged her. She pulled back.

"But Hansje—"

There it was, the all too familiar *but*.

"You're not naive, so don't act like it," Pien said. "Why would we want to go to a place where they burned down a synagogue last spring?"

———————

Keeping a positive spirit became more and more difficult. It was a miserably cloudy morning. Ab, Nico, and I were sitting in our living room. Ab was drinking tea whilst I was sewing a Yellow Star of David on his coat.

Since April, there had been a rule stating that it was illegal for Jews not to wear the symbol which, in its centre, had the word *Jood* embroidered on it, meaning Jew.

"Why are we supposed to identify ourselves? I thought those German rats said they could smell a Jew from miles away," Ab slurped his tea and spilled some on his clean shirt. "And we also have to pay for them!"

Nico was holding Betty, who was now seven months old.

Ab looked at Betty with admiration and concern. "That kid doesn't even know the half of what's waiting for her."

"If anyone dares to come near my child, I'll scratch their eyes out."

"Don't be catty," Ab said.

"Hansje!" Nico was surprised. My brother was used to my occasional spiteful remarks, but I tried to remain calm whenever Nico was around. But before I could apologise, Nico smiled and said, "I do have to agree with you on that one."

I held out Ab's coat and presented the embroidered star to him.

"All done." He thanked me.

I looked at the clock.

"Oh god, it's past four o'clock and I haven't had time to go to the shops yet. I'm sure the cues will be too long for me to do the shopping in time!" I grabbed my bag in a hurry. "Can you look after Betty?" Nico nodded.

"Wait," he said, and I went back to give him a kiss. *A kiss for good luck*. It was our thing to make sure we kiss before leaving one another. No matter what day, time, or on what occasion, we would always have that little gesture.

On my way out, I saw Bonneka, who was carrying a couple of shopping bags. I kissed both her cheeks and told her I was in a hurry.

"Hansje, you won't make it in time! Bring my groceries to your flat and tell me what I should get you."

"You are an angel," I grabbed both her bags, "Just some milk, eggs, and white fish if you can find it." I gave Bonneka a few guilders and my rationing card. She nodded and went off.

"That was quick." Nico was still holding Betty when I got back inside. "Two hours we have! Only two hours to buy groceries. They're insane," Ab complained.

"Next time I'll go to the kosher store," I said.

"They haven't got anything, and I don't think it's a good idea to be walking around the Jewish Quarter by yourself." Ab was right.

When Bonneka came back from the store, Ab had left for work. She entered the apartment with a small shopping bag. I thanked her. Nico was wearing a shirt with an embroidered Yellow David star symbol. Bonneka took a quick peek at the star and shook her head. "Nol is coming home next Wednesday," she said. "Just for a couple of weeks. You both should come over for dinner."

It was illegal for Jews to visit non-Jews, but we were neighbours and had been friends since before all of those rules were implemented.

"We would love to," I said, hugging her. Bonneka took her bags, and once she had closed the door behind her, Nico said, "I don't think that's a good idea. There are snitches everywhere."

"Practically everyone in the building knows us. No one will make a fuss."

"They'll smile to your face and rat you out behind your back."

"Are you worried?" I asked humbly. He didn't respond. "Are you scared?"

"Scared?" Nico gazed at me for a moment and then smiled. "As long as I have you and Betty and I know you're okay, how could I be?"

It didn't answer my question.

Nico and I hadn't been intimate for a very long time. Probably not since before Betty was born. It wasn't just because of our lack of privacy or having to take care of the baby. We had an unspoken fear of what would happen if I were to get pregnant again. Now was definitely not the time to have a second child. I did enjoy the thought of considering it, when things would go back to normal. I often daydreamed about all those possibilities: Nico being able to get a better job, and moving to a house of our own, maybe even one that has two or three bedrooms. Perhaps even a house in the suburbs. But for now, those thoughts seemed all too far away.

"Do you know what Ab told me?" Nico said.

My brother often did this. Whenever Ab didn't have the courage to tell me something, he would say it to Nico instead, knowing that we discussed everything.

"What is it?"

He looked down and rubbed his face, as though he was second guessing himself.

"What?" I asked again.

"He told me about the disappearances."

"What do you mean, disappearances?"

"Some families have been disappearing into thin air."

I had heard about the work camps in the north-east of the country. "It's not just that. Some younger couples sent letters to their families saying that they're being sent to the East for work."

"That's not so far away."

"Not the East in the Netherlands, Eastern Europe! These people's families haven't heard anything from them for months," Nico emphasised. I remembered when the Jewish council had first started explaining these work camps in our country, but Eastern Europe? That made me slightly more worried.

"That Abraham Asscher is a spineless traitor," I said. "But do you really think he would try to kill his own people?"

"That guy would do anything to save his own skin."

"I doubt we will be sent away."

"But what if we will?" Nico raised his voice. There was something that I hadn't yet told Nico.

"Trust me, there might be something that—"

"Stop it, you don't know anything!" I froze. Nico rarely acted this way.

"Look around you. Strangers are deciding our future for us, and there is nothing we can do about it."

"We're exempt," I blurted out.

"What?"

"I got a letter, from my old work. The Jewish Council is granting some of the key irreplaceable employees a *Sperre*."

"What's that?"

"I'll show you." I opened a drawer and took out an envelope. He grabbed it and hastily read the document.

"An official delay of execution . . . Is this for the both of us?"

"I wouldn't accept this if it wasn't."

"So, what do we do now?"

"We go get some stamps on our identity cards and stay in Amsterdam."

"And they granted *you* this?"

I was trying not to feel offended, but I knew exactly what Nico meant. I had left school at an early age to go work, and even during my younger years, I wasn't necessarily the best student. Nevertheless, my position in the firm was an important one. I had knowledge about the diamond industry thanks to my family, who used to be highly qualified professionals, my administrative skills were notable, and becoming an office worker and accountant required many years of training.

"Difficult to replace in the short term," Nico argued. "Have you thought about what would happen to Betty?"

She was on the floor, holding a wooden shaker. She was a clever and stubborn child. She could babble on for minutes on end, as if telling a structureless story with only sounds and claps. And when

Betty wasn't happy about something, she always found a way to show it. I looked at my baby, who was playing with her toys and giggling.

"I will ruin anyone who comes near my child," I said without a doubt.

"So, Betty will also receive a stamp, right?" Nico asked.

"Maybe it's best if we leave Betty out of the equation, keep her on the down low."

He understood my thinking but seemed to have something going on in his own mind. Sometimes I wished I could just read his thoughts, know what was going on in that brain of his.

"Ab thinks that when the summer's over, we'll all have to go into hiding," he finally said.

"I'm sure Ab is eligible for the *Sperre*. He can get a stamp too." After all, my brother and I had similar qualifications.

But that made me think about my father. Regardless of his knowledge and expertise, he was barely capable of remembering how to tie his shoelaces. Was Ab going to leave him in the psychiatric hospital without anyone taking care of him? The thought angered me.

Nico could sense my frustration and put his hand on my shoulder. He sighed. "We'll hold on for a little longer, thanks to you. And maybe you're right and things could be looking up sooner than we imagine."

———————

But in the autumn, things had only gotten worse. I hadn't seen Pien for a while. It was difficult to see friends due to the eight o'clock curfew. I didn't see much of father or Ab either. Taking care of Betty was a full-time job, the weather was getting colder, and we barely had any heating left in the house.

"It's been a while since we've heard anything from Bonneka." Nico was trying to heat up the little bit of coal we had left.

"Probably because Nol is back in town," I said, though I realised there was something else going on. I tried to keep my suspicions from Nico. The last few months had been a little peculiar in our neighbourhood. The people who we had been friends with before now completely ignored our existence. It seemed as if they all had an unspoken agreement to bully us away. Bonneka and Nol had always been very close to us, so I couldn't ever imagine them turning against us. But, on the other hand, I felt foolish for my compulsory cheerfulness. Every day, I became more and more stunned by how cruel some people could be.

"Bonneka will pop by at some point, and if not, then we just won't hear from her," I said, trying to sound detached.

Nico nodded. He put on his coat, gave me a kiss for good luck, and went to work. Once he had left, I put Betty in her pram. It felt like a daily challenge to go outside. I decided that I would just put up with the discriminating looks and finally go for a long walk. I stepped outside and saw Doortje and Klaas across the street. Just the people I wanted to avoid. Doortje gave me a subtle smile and Klaas looked at me as if I were a stranger. At least I got one smile. That was more than I would get most days.

"Hansje!" Ab called me from the corner of the street. He was wearing his long brown coat with the embroidered Yellow Star. For a brief moment, he looked happy to see me, until his facial expression changed to one of distress.

I kissed both his cheeks, and he slid a letter in my hand.

"Let's go for a walk," he said, and he took over the pram. We walked in silence for a while, trying to avoid crowded areas where there were too many people. Eventually we found a path next to the river where we could quietly promenade. I looked at the letter in my hand; it seemed to be one of the Jewish Council. I opened it discreetly and read.

L.S.

The German authorities have informed us that within the next month, you must leave your home and move to the address on the other side of this letter. If you do not agree with this course of action, your other option is to report for voluntary immigration.

Upon moving to your new home, you are allowed to take as much luggage as each family member can carry.

You must fill out an enclosed form with the contents that you will take with you, and hand it to the homeowners upon arrival.

The German authorities warn that those who refuse this order shall be issued for arrest (Schutzhäftlinge).

Yours sincerely,

The Jewish Council of Amsterdam.

"Voluntary immigration, is this a joke? Where are they moving us to?"

"Ben Viljoenstraat," Ab said as he lit up a cigarette.

"Shove us all into the Jewish Quarter."

"It's easier to monitor us when we live in a concentrated area. But at least we're not being sent to Drenthe."

He seemed unusually calm.

A couple of German soldiers passed by and looked at us. One of them spat on the floor and another one shouted. "*Pferdezähne!*" Horse teeth.

Over the last couple of weeks, I had been scared to go out on the street by myself, and this was an example of why. Even though the officers knew they could bully me in any way they wanted, as long as there was a man next to me, they usually wouldn't come any closer.

"Ignore them," Ab said, and he took back the letter.

We walked across the Amstel River and passed by a bench with a sign that said *Forbidden for Jews*. Ab would usually take off his coat and sit on these benches to make a statement, but for some reason, he seemed more cautious today.

We walked across the river in complete silence. I was waiting for him to say something—Ab always had something to say. He didn't even comment on what the soldiers had said, which was unusual for my quick-witted brother.

I licked my front teeth. The only other time I had ever been called horse teeth was by Frans Engelstein in primary school. It felt hurtful back then, though at least I had had the confidence and courage to stand up for myself. Hearing the soldiers make this remark was so much worse. Not only was I a grown-up woman, but there was absolutely nothing I could say. When I was a kid, it hurt because I wanted to be pretty like all the other girls. Now it hurt because those soldiers didn't care how I looked—they would think of me as worthless either way.

"Stop licking your teeth," Ab had noticed, and I felt embarrassed. I tried to change the subject.

"Have you told father about the letter?" I asked.

Ab sighed and didn't respond. We continued walking, until he finally said, "I have been trying to get father out of Apeldoornse Bos. But there's something going on there, shady things."

"What kind of shady things?" I asked, worried.

"I don't know for sure, but what I do know is that Mozes needs to get the hell out of there."

In a way, I felt ignorant for not knowing about most of the things going on around me, but I was also trying to protect myself. The fear of knowing what was happening could prevent me from taking care of Betty and making sure she was raised in a safe and loving environment.

"There is something else you should know," Ab stopped me and looked around, making sure there was no one nearby. Betty started crying, and I took her out of the pram.

"Shush her!" Ab said, trying to make sure no attention was drawn to us.

Betty was still crying.

A group of young teenage boys approached us.

"Make sure that devil's baby shuts the fuck up!" They all laughed.

Ab could see my anger and turned me away from them.

"I'm so sorry, guys. We'll move out of your way," he threw away his cigarette on the floor and grabbed my arm.

I couldn't believe it. Ab was letting them have their way. I put Betty, who had quietened down, back in the pram and looked at the boys. They were probably fifteen years old.

"What did you just say about my child?" I shouted back. Ab made a disapproving sound.

"That he'll probably grow up as ugly as you," said the smallest one.

"Hansje, let's go," Ab said, desperately trying to leave the situation. The guys came closer, and Betty started crying again. I felt such anger but realised I was just giving them what they wanted. I didn't care if they would do anything to me, but I suddenly felt an intense fear that they could harm Betty. I looked at Ab, already retreating and taking the pram with him.

"Hansje!" he shouted.

The boys were waiting for me to react. I just tried to keep my mouth shut and joined Ab. We left there as quickly as we could.

"You people grow like fungus, and it makes Amsterdam smell," said another boy. They all laughed, working each other up. "Give our country and money back and leave!"

We rushed back to our flat. On the way, I got upset at Ab.

"What happened to you?" I asked.

He laughed indifferently. "LML," he said—a Dutch expression, which he couldn't get enough of. *Laat maar lullen*: let them talk crap.

As much as I didn't like going outside, Ab didn't like being inside. He had a huge fear of the *Ordnungspolizei*[2] breaking in at any given moment. To some of his friends, this had recently happened, and the more it occurred, the more anxious Ab would be.

"What did you want to tell me earlier?"

---

2 ***Ordungspolizei*** were the uniformed regular police force responsible for maintaining public order in Nazi-occupied Europe.

Ab was nervously fiddling with his fingers.

"I have some news," he said. "I'm going into hiding."

It all suddenly started feeling more real. The looks, the threats, the rules—it had been going on for so long that it had become my new reality. Though I always hoped it wouldn't come to this.

"Where?"

He wasn't allowed to tell me, but he whispered that Bonneka was taking care of it for him.

"Bonneka?" I asked confusedly.

"Yes, didn't you know?" Ab said, "Bonneka and Nol are part of the resistance."

WINTER, LATE 1942

ON MY TWENTY-NINTH BIRTHDAY, we went to visit my father in the psychiatric hospital, Apeldoornse Bos. I tried to shake off a horrible feeling which was constantly in my mind. *What if this were to be the last time that I would ever see my father again?* He was weaker, thinner, and more unhappy than I had ever seen him. Ab had tried everything to get him out of that place, but to no avail.

"I have been speaking to the doctors, the administration office, and even threatened to go to court. You'll be back home in no time," he said to father.

"Don't worry about me. Take care of yourselves first. And especially of your little treasure."

By then, my beautiful baby daughter was already eleven months old. She had an adventurous side, crawling everywhere and attempting to walk a couple of steps without our help. Betty also loved it when I played piano. I would spend hours playing, and she would just sit next to me, listen to the melodies, and dance out of rhythm. Unfortunately, our new home in the Ben Viljoenstraat didn't have a piano. It was the thing I felt most regretful leaving behind.

"Take care of Betty," father repeated once more.

We got back home later that day. The flat was very small, even smaller than our crowded place at the Lekstraat. At least we knew everyone in our street and had genuine friendly relations with them.

Most people had come to congratulate me on my birthday, and some presented us with lovely home-cooked dishes. Feline and Boaz, our next-door neighbours gave me a dried fruitcake.

"It isn't much," Feline said, "but very easy to make. My secret ingredient is to use black tea instead of butter."

"You're spoiling me, thank you."

Their efforts and warmth already made me feel happier about living there. Though, one of the people I was mostly missing on this day was Bonneka, who always baked us treats.

When we finished eating the cake, Ab stood up to hug me.

"Happy birthday, big sister," he said.

At least we had each other. That thought made me happy.

Ab picked up Betty who was giggling. "And you, little B, are the best present your mum could have ever wished for."

Nico gave me a kiss, and I loved the feeling of his cold lips pressed against mine.

"Happy birthday, beautiful," he said tenderly. Nico wasn't the romantic type, though he tried. But it made his little moments of affection even more special.

"One day we'll have it all," I said.

"I already have everything I want," he said. I turned away to hide my coy look and red cheeks. Boaz playfully pushed Nico's shoulder.

"There they are, those charms," Boaz smirked. "I was starting to wonder how you got your wife to fall for you."

Feline giggled. She loved it when Boaz was loud and inappropriate. It almost felt like a normal birthday. Almost. I tried to forget that

Ab would be leaving us fairly soon. His Sperre stamp didn't seem to matter anymore, seeing as he had been summoned to go to the work camps in Drenthe. Apparently, they needed strong men. I didn't believe this to be as harmful as he was implying, though Ab disagreed. "Why would they need me for manual labour? I'm much better with my brains," he would say. So, the only option left for him was to go into hiding. He had made arrangements with Bonneka and told me to do the same, before things would get more difficult. The Jewish Council had been sending these letters to more and more individuals and families in our neighbourhood. We realised that these were being sent in an alphabetical order. Thanks to my married surname, which starts with an M, Nico and I hadn't received a letter just yet. My maiden name, and Ab's current surname, started with a C. Even so, we weren't all too sure, given that Ab had been asked to leave for manual labour. It would probably take another while before we'd receive a letter, I hoped.

Pien was in hiding now, too, but she had managed to still send me a birthday card. I wondered how she was doing, and how her children, Harry and Evi, were. I missed them. Nostalgically, I thought back to the time when we were free. When we would go dancing, out in town, biking through the city. Even though I was only twenty-nine, the stress of the past year had manifested itself onto my physique. It scared me every time I looked in the mirror to see the bags under my eyes, another wrinkle or a few white hairs appear. Nico would tell me I was being ridiculous, though I knew that he saw it too.

"So long, Hansje," Ab said, hugging us goodbye.

"Until soon, promise me that." I hugged him tightly, almost unwilling to let him go.

"I promise," Ab said, and he left.

———————

Jan 21, 1943

Dear children,

Today, I am writing this letter to you because we have been told that we must all leave Appeldoornsche Bos. No one knows where to.

Assumably, you are aware of the struggles that we have been experiencing the past few days. My nurse, Arnold, who has been by my side for all this time, will tell you all that you need to know.

Hansje, fourteen days ago, you sent me a card in which you wrote that I should stay strong and hold my head up high. Now, dear Ab and Hansje, I have been doing just that, holding my head up high. I will still stay strong, and if the good God allows me to be well, I hope to see you soon.

Give little B lots of kisses from me. I'll always think of you.

Your father

I read the letter twelve times, not knowing what to do. I wish I could've taken a bike ride to wherever Ab was and talk to him. Often, I would disregard his pessimistic and overly rational ideas, but now I was longing for those opinions. If only I could just go and see father, or Ab, or anyone who could be of help.

Betty was on my lap whilst I was rereading the letter a thirteenth time. She was now more than a year old and had lost all of her chubby baby rolls. I had been so scared of underfeeding her, and now she was looking leaner than she had for the past few months. I knew it was because she was growing older, but that did not stop me from worrying.

Betty babbled.

"Ab tried so hard to get him out," I said to her. My arms were shaking. I lifted Betty off my lap and put her on the floor. My head became so heavy. I tried to focus on a single point in the room, not letting the chills take over my body. My eyes were watering, blurring my vision. I looked at Betty, observing her every move, but could not stop myself from getting intrusive thoughts—about what would happen if we had to leave Amsterdam ourselves, and what could happen to her.

There was a muffled sound of keys rumbling outside the front door, and Nico entered the flat. He could see that something was wrong, so he dropped everything and ran to hug me.

"Have you heard about the transport?" There was an anxious tone in Nico's voice.

I nodded.

"Five families have already left!"

I didn't know what he was talking about.

He showed me another letter. It was similar to the one Ab gave me a couple of months ago. Nico told me they had been sending families in our street the same letter, which implied that they would have to go live and work in the east of the country.

I rubbed my face and tried to regain composure. "We need to speak to Bonneka."

In my head, I could hear two voices, Ab's and my own. The two extremes of our relationship. On the one hand, I had a recurring thought of wanting to pack a small bag with food, water, and clothes, put Betty in her pram, and leave the flat for good. Our first stop would be Apeldoornse Bos, to pick up father. I was imagining what I'd say to them. "He is an intelligent, capable, and respected family man. You made a mistake, and we will leave with him, whether you will allow it or not." Then we would look for Ab, and the five of us would stay at Bonneka's apartment for a little while. Father would sit down in the brown leather chair, drinking a glass of milk with some butter biscuits. He would be happy to see Betty crawling around the apartment, humming the tunes of the songs she remembers me playing. Ab, Nico, and I would be sitting at Bonneka's dinner table, and all of us would be discussing the next course of action. Where we should go and how we would get there. Leave Amsterdam and go to New York, London, or even Jerusalem.

And yet, all I could hear was Ab's voice telling me that I was being ridiculous, that I need to stay calm, be smart. Hold my head up high but keep on the down low. Going into hiding was the safer option for everyone, and we shouldn't seek dangerous and unnecessary contact.

I explained both these thoughts to Nico, not revealing that the second one came from Ab's voice. Without thinking, Nico grabbed a pencil and some paper.

"All right," he said, "I will send a letter to Bonneka and Nol, asking for their help."

———————————

A week later, there was a knock on our door.

I opened it and, to my surprise, I saw Nol standing there. He gave me three kisses.

"It's so nice to see you," I said, and he reacted a little vigilant.

"Would you like to come visit us later this afternoon?" he asked. Before I could respond, he continued, "Just make sure you hide your Yellow Star when you do visit. Try to avoid others, especially Klaas. If you were to cross anyone, just tell them that you had to pick up something of Betty's which you forgot."

Later that day, I asked our neighbour, Feline, whether she could take care of Betty for the afternoon. She gladly accepted and didn't ask any questions. No one in our neighbourhood ever did.

Nico and I left the flat and walked all the way to the Lekstraat, where we used to live. Nothing about the place had changed, except that it didn't feel like our home anymore. No one was around, but we both still sensed the tense atmosphere of our presence there.

The tension quickly diminished when we entered Bonneka and Nol's apartment, which was enriched by a smell of baked goods. On the table, she had a selection of star shaped jam-filled biscuits, as well as gingerbread cake and pear-filled brioche buns.

"Where did you get all of this food?" I wondered. I hadn't been able to buy full-fat dairy products or eggs for almost a year. The places where I went only had watery milk and old cheese. "Jam and sugar?" I was amazed. "The whole building will know you've been baking with this smell. It isn't how you keep things discreet."

Bonneka gestured that we should sit down.

"Don't worry, the neighbours often smell this. They think it's for the Gestapo," Bonneka said. "Have as much as you want."

Whilst we were eating the biscuits, she went away and came back with some documents which she lay onto the table in two different piles. Nico and I got curious. We stopped indulging in the biscuits and tried to guess what was written on those documents.

"I have been in contact with your brother," she said.

"You've seen Ab?"

"No, we've been writing."

"Have you heard about Mozes?" I asked, and Bonneka shook her head. I gave her the letter he had sent. Bonneka took a quick look and gave it back. She seemed disturbed, but not surprised.

Bonneka pointed at one of the piles of documents on the table. "This is where you'll be hiding."

Nico hunched over and, without touching the paper, scammed through the first page of both piles.

"Why are there two different addresses? Do we have to choose where we want to go?" he asked.

"Of course not! It's not a hotel."

I grabbed the ticker pile and thoroughly read it. There was some information about a seemingly large family with an address in North Amsterdam. Then I put it down and read the other document, including information about a married woman whose husband lived abroad.

There wasn't much information, apart from the fact that she had no children and that she lived in South Amsterdam.

"We're going to be separated, aren't we?"

Bonneka answered honestly. "It's the safest option."

Nico turned to face me but kept quiet. I couldn't look at him. He took both my hands and squeezed them firmly.

"Hiding inside a basement is no life for a baby," Bonneka said.

"How do we know that this family will take good care of her?"

"They are honest people, hard workers, and we have checked all that we can about them."

"Still, they have many children. How will I know for certain that they'll take good care of Betty?"

"You won't."

That wasn't what I wanted to hear. I let go of Nico's hands and stood up.

"Will you excuse me for a moment?"

I went to the bathroom and leaned over the sink. My heart was pounding out of my chest. Ab's voice in my head was telling me it was the right decision. Though I still wanted to write him a letter and hear his actual advice. There was no time for that.

I went back into the living room.

Nico had taken off his glasses and was running his hands through his hair. He turned to me as I sat down again. He placed his hand on the back of my neck and leaned forward. We touched foreheads, and I could feel the warmth of his breath as it accelerated.

"I don't mean to interrupt, but we're pressed for time," Bonneka said bluntly.

Nico kissed my cheek. I sat back up and straightened myself out. "Tell us what we have to do."

We left Bonneka's place separately, not to create a stir. I closed the door behind me and walked onto the pavement, then I saw Klaas, who was walking on the opposite side of the street. There were two men with him, both tall, one bald guy and the other one a redhead with a beard. I was trying to keep my head low, hoping they wouldn't notice me. We locked eyes, and it was clear that we were both unhappy to see each other. I hoped that he would ignore me, but he crossed the street and his friends followed.

"You shouldn't be here," he said casually.

"Excuse me?"

"What are you doing here?"

Klaas had never been this blunt with me. I knew his opinions about our family had drastically changed in the last couple of years, but he now spoke to me as if I had been a nuisance for all those years. The dreadful neighbours who made too much noise and left a mess around the building.

"I just came to pick something up. I won't happen again," I said, trying to leave the conversation.

"Do me a favour," he came so close that I could smell the liquor on his breath. "Don't ever come back here to manipulate Doortje. She might be soft and gullible, but I know what you people really want."

I wanted to say, *Respect and freedom. That is the only thing we want.* But knew I had to hold in my anger or else I would just prove his point. I gave a gentle nod and said, "You won't see me around."

Klaas thanked me with a broad grin, but his words had stung like acidic venom. It was unreal that after years of being friendly with one another, I was now the pest that he wanted to protect his family from. I quickly walked off, though I could still vaguely hear his friends, cheering him up, as if he were a brave man who did what he had to do.

———————

One early morning in March, when the sun hadn't fully risen yet, I was packing a small bag with some of Betty's things: her rattle toys, a pair of tiny snakeskin leather shoes (which I had worn as a toddler), a plush toy rabbit, my scarf, Nico's gloves, and a locket with our pictures. "It's going to be an adventure," I said to little Betty, who was giggling and crawling around the flat. I hadn't eaten that morning and still felt my stomach turn. After I finished putting everything in the bag, I loaded it into the pram and sat down next to Betty. She was on the floor, looking at me with squinted dark brown eyes. We sat in silence for a couple of minutes, staring at each other, as if she could read my mind and knew what was happening. Then she started crying. I took her in my arms and cradled her. She was getting bigger and heavier, and I found myself become slightly weaker, but at least I could still hold her in my arms. After a moment, she stopped crying and grabbed my little finger.

Nico came out of the bathroom and looked at us. I could see that he had been crying too, even though this was something he would never admit. He came towards us, took Betty under her armpits, and picked her up, out of my lap.

"I hope that one day you will be as brave, as smart, and as kind as your mother."

I got up and softly caressed his cheek, though he turned his head the other way. Betty said, 'Dada,' and I nodded. "Yes, that is your dada; never forget that." She looked a little confused and responded with "bye-bye."

Nico gave Betty one last kiss and put her back in my arms. He lifted her pram, opened the door of the flat, and carried the pram all the way downstairs. When he came back up, he avoided looking me in the eyes, went into the bedroom, and closed the door behind him.

"Nico, please—"

I couldn't bear going out and doing this without our usual kiss for good luck. Though, the clock was ticking, and I would have to leave fairly soon. I was still holding Betty, but I knocked on the bedroom door.

"Nico?"

"Dada," said Betty.

"Come out please."

There was no response, and I had to leave. I put Betty's coat on and went outside, without locking the door behind me.

Secretly I was hoping that someone would have stolen the pram, but when I came downstairs holding Betty, it was still there. I gently put her inside and began walking.

I wanted this walk to last forever, but I tried to focus on Betty and my surroundings. I had to be extremely cautious and make sure I made no mistakes. When I got out of the Jewish Quarter, I moved my scarf slightly over the embroidered Yellow Star, hiding it as much as I could. It was illegal not to wear the star, and I could be in big trouble if someone found out I was trying to hide it. From what I had learned over the past few months, there were snitches everywhere, especially those you wouldn't expect it from. On the other side of the river, there was a mother walking with her two children. They threw rocks into the river, and I was hoping she hadn't noticed the star on my coat. She didn't seem to be eyeing me, so I moved along.

Finally, after walking for half an hour, I arrived on the corner of two streets, where Bonneka had instructed me to wait. I tried to remember what she had told me. *Make sure no one is following you, don't look suspicious, cover your Yellow Star . . .* Those were the easier ones. Now came the hard part. *Once you arrive at the corner of those two streets, you will have to make sure no one is watching you, leave the pram, and slowly walk away. Don't let Betty see you walking away, or she'll start crying.*

The pram was a ticking time-bomb, ready to explode any minute, and I had to get out of there—though all of my instincts were telling me to stay. I couldn't even give her one last kiss. So, I did exactly what Bonneka had told me to. I walked away.

Every step away from the pram felt like a stab in my chest. I tried walking at a normal pace; yet, I could not help but slowing down the further I got. I was trying not to cry, as it would only seem suspicious. All of my instincts were telling me to stop. I was now almost out of sight. And then it hit me—I had to go back. I turned around but was too far away to see the pram. At a quick pace, I went back, not even thinking about whether anyone would see me. My steps were heavy, and my shoulders were hunched over.

The pram was back in sight. And there was someone standing next to it. A woman, slightly older than me, wearing a ragged coat and worn out shoes, holding an umbrella. She took over Betty's pram as though it was the most normal thing in the world. Bonneka had told me not to turn around, and I felt guilty. I looked away and leaned against a nearby tree. I still had the urge to run and bring my baby back home with me, but I felt foolish. Or at least I wanted to speak to the lady who would take care of my little girl—making sure she would do all that was necessary.

I regretted not leaving a note for her, to explain some things. Bonneka forbade it, but it wouldn't have made such a difference. In the note, I would've written:

Betty likes listening to classical music, preferably on the piano, and to shake her rattle in tune with the music. If you give her mushed up vegetables, she'll spit it out, but she'll eat the bite-sized cooked pieces. Betty is a smart baby but needs a little bit of discipline when it comes to her stubbornness. Give her hugs and rewards for being kind. We will be back soon.

I had to get home. It was too early for Jews to be walking around town. But I couldn't get myself to move away from the tree. After a few minutes, I tried to remind myself of all the good things Bonneka had told me about the family that was going to take care of Betty.

They were the Bloem family, who lived in North Amsterdam. Mr. Bloem was a plumber, and his wife, Mrs. Bloem, had been a seamstress at Gerzon, a well-known Jewish department store. They lived in a very small house and had four children. This family was willing to take Betty into their home, which put the whole family at risk if they got caught. The family had seen pictures of Betty and decided that they would tell everyone that they had adopted a child from the Dutch East Indies, a colony in South-East Asia. Betty's skin was slightly darker than that of Dutch children, which was why this could seem like a good excuse.

When I arrived back home, Nico came to hug me. We hugged for a very long time. He asked how she was doing, and I told him that our little Betty didn't make a sound. "She's strong, our little one," I said. "She'll survive."

There were no more blankets of hers I could smell or no pictures to look at. Everything was either with Bonneka or thrown away. If we were to get caught, we had to make sure that no SS soldier would ever know a baby had lived in this apartment.

That evening, we sat at the dinner table in silence. We hadn't said a full sentence to one another since this morning.

"The stew is delicious." Nico tried to make conversation. My eyes gazed down at the stockpot on the table, which was filled with some watery mash of spinach and potato. I couldn't swallow one bite and played around with the food on my plate.

Nico stopped eating. He leaned back and licked his lips. His long sigh was one I recognised every time something was wrong.

"Someone came to pick her up. We shouldn't worry about her."

Nico muttered a sound. There was something else going on. He took a scrunched-up letter out of his pocket.

"I wasn't going to show you this tonight."

"What is it?"

He handed me the letter. It had the insignia of the Jewish Council, which usually wasn't positive. I started reading it and Nico interrupted. "Our Sperre status will soon be abolished. We're being sent to the work camps in Drenthe."

I closed my eyes and took a deep breath.

"It's our turn to go into hiding."

———————

Every day, I checked the mailbox to see whether any letters from Bonneka had arrived. She hadn't been in contact with us for a couple of weeks, which made us worry.

"What should we do?" Nico asked. "Send her more money?"

The woman who Bonneka had made arrangements with was being difficult. She wanted more money from the people who wanted to go into hiding now that the stakes were getting higher.

"We can't pay her. Most of our savings have been taken to who knows where."

"There might be another option," Nico said. He showed me a postcard from Artis, a zoo in the heart of Amsterdam.

"You want to go to the zoo?" I said sarcastically. Not that we could. We weren't allowed to go there anymore.

Nico flipped the postcard, which had writings on it.

"Boaz and Feline are going there," he said, "I wasn't allowed to tell you this until they left."

Nico explained everything that Boaz had told him. Apparently, he used to work at Artis as a young boy, years before the war even started. He knew the place inside and out. Him and Feline even went to visit in 1942, regardless of the fact that the zoo had a sign saying *Forbidden for Jews.*

Nico said more light-heartedly, "Boaz says that the sign is just there to flatter the Germans and the NSB; they never actually check any of the visitors."

Boaz and Feline were an adventurous couple. I wish I had known them sooner. The last weeks had been more bearable thanks to their presence. They managed to bring a sort of lightness to most situations, especially when things were tough. Though they still struggled. Feline had lost a lot of weight. One day, she showed me pictures of what she used to look like before the war. She wasn't as curvaceous anymore and her luscious blond hair had become thinner and crisper. But that didn't take away her charm. Quite the opposite, Boaz loved her very much and joked that the less attractive she became, the more her personality shone.

"So Feline and Boaz are going into hiding at Artis?"

He showed me the postcard. It didn't really make sense.

"Boaz wrote it in code," Nico explained, "Everything we need to know is in there."

I took the card and started reading, trying to understand the puzzle.

March 30, 1943

Dearest friends,

Our time at Artis has been wonderful. The kind zookeeper, Peter, lend us his green hat, which we still have to give back. Flora is over the moon. He even allowed us through the back door to go see the monkeys. I told him how much I enjoy going to see the monkeys. If you ever go and visit, tell him that you're a friend of mine. We hope to see you soon! All the best,

Bert and Flora

I guessed. "Go to the back door, find Peter with the green hat, and tell him we're Boaz's friends."

"Very close. We also need to explain that we want to see the monkeys."

"We can't hide in a zoo."

"But it won't take long before we get a letter from the Jewish Council."

"Bonneka won't know where to find us."

"Then let's send her this postcard."

Nico was right. Every night, we lay wide awake, afraid that the police would break down our door to arrest us and take us away.

"Let's give it two more weeks. Bonneka might be in touch with us soon."

Nico imposed, "If we get a letter from the Jewish Council by then, we leave."

SPRING, 1943

NICO AND I were strolling along the Amstel River. It had been a couple of months since we last saw Betty. Still, her presence was constantly on my mind. I wondered how she was integrating in her temporary family, if she had learned any new words, whether she was eating well, and how they were raising her. Nico could almost hear my thoughts. "Hansje, I'm sure she's in good hands."

But it wasn't just that. I wasn't just worried about whether they were taking good care of Betty. I trusted Bonneka and knew she would put her somewhere safe. What worried me was to know that Betty was growing up without her parents by her side. What if, one day, I picked her up after the war, and she didn't remember me? What if she'd cry to her new mother, asking who those strangers were, coming to take her away?

I was trying to brush over the topic. I didn't like speaking about Betty, as it reminded me of the day I left her on that street corner.

Even the happy memories were difficult. They often included Ab and my father, whose absence I painfully felt. They were two of the most important people in my life, and I had no way of communicating with them or knowing where they were. All I could do was write Ab letters, and hope that they would arrive. Bonneka told me where I should send them so that they would arrive to Ab safely, without anyone being able to trace our whereabouts. I had asked Bonneka about the family we would stay with, though she said that it was better to keep that information quiet for now. So, I had asked if she could tell me more about Ab's hiding place.

She told me, "He's staying with two ladies, Moor and Hansje."

"Hansje, just like me," I said happily, knowing that it would remind Ab of his big sister.

"Not only Ab, though. A couple of others are hiding there too."

"Those women must be brave. Living their lives helping others. It's such a big secret, and they could get caught any day."

"That's not the only thing that they're hiding."

"I'm not following."

Bonneka laughed. "You're a progressive woman, Hansje. You'll figure it out."

Nico held my hand. We used to be an amorous couple, but this had lessened over the years. And yet, now was the time when we needed each other's comfort the most. I glanced at the flowing river, which glistened in the sunlight's reflection. A slight breeze brushed over us, and my hand felt the cold touch of Nico's fingers. I always complained about how cold his hands and feet were, but today, whilst the sun was shining on our skin, his cold touch felt pleasant.

I studied his face, remembering the day I fell for him.

It was in the summer of '36. For years, my group of girlfriends and I went to the tennis court on Sundays. My best friends were Pien, Beb, Lea, Selma, and Lientje. We would bike there in the morning and spend the whole day playing. Then, to reward ourselves, we would spend evenings in the tennis court cafe. It was always full of fellow tennis players, who we had become acquainted with over the years. Even years later, after some of the girls had gotten married, we still kept this Sunday tradition. Though, sometimes, Pien brought her husband Henry and I would bring Ab. And his friends, Leo and Frank, would often come along too. On one occasion, Frank even brought his cousin with him.

A handsome guy with slicked-back hair and small round glasses, just a couple of years older than me. This guy seemed like a well-groomed intellectual, and I couldn't wait to see him fail at tennis. It turned out I wasn't wrong. The men were playing a singles match and Frank and his cousin had teamed up against Leo and Henry. Us girls were sitting down, judging the match from afar and sipping our small bottles of lemonade. The fact that these men had a female audience made them even more nervous, which we enjoyed thoroughly. I especially liked watching Frank's cousin play.

He picked up his tennis racket, barely knowing where to grip it. He threw the ball in the air and missed his first serve. He probably realised that we were watching him, which made the poor guy even more nervous. He missed his second serve too, and after this double fault, their match would assumably be over quite quickly.

"Have you met him before?" Pien asked.

I giggled. "I probably would've remembered those terrible glasses!" Pien tapped my leg, embarrassed by my behaviour.

I was lying, of course. Not only had I met this man, but I remembered him very well. Our fathers used to attend the same Sabbath morning readings a couple of decades ago. And our mothers enjoyed the occasional gossip at synagogue. Though, sadly, this hadn't lasted for very long, as both his parents passed away at a very young age due to illness.

I fancied him when we were kids. Every time he passed by our neighbourhood, he was always crossing the road holding a newspaper. Then a decade later, he was introduced at my office as a new employee. One of the traveling salesmen. Even though we had different jobs and he was often away, I made an effort to see him whenever he was around. And his name was Nathan. At the office, he was a quiet man, always walking around the building holding a newspaper, just like when he was a kid. It wasn't that I didn't dare to go up to him and chat—I just always thought a man should make the first move in that kind of situation.

He never did. He barely even noticed my existence. Though I was sure he must have known my name. After all, no one's a stranger for long in the Jewish community in Amsterdam. I just hoped he wasn't engaged to someone else.

When the boys finished their match, Frank introduced this *mysterious* highbrow man to the group.

"My cousin, Nathan."

They weren't related by blood; I knew. Probably fourth cousins or so.

"Everyone calls me Nico."

Selma held out her hand. "Nice to see you play, Nico."

"It would've been nice if we'd *actually* seen you play," I teased. He seemed quite taken aback.

"This is the second match I've ever played."

"You're a natural."

He gave a chuckle.

"Some have got good brains, others good sport."

"I imagine you've got both."

"Touché."

I was pleasantly surprised by his sudden engagement.

After that day, we finally started socialising at the office. He was luckily not just an acquaintance anymore. But I stood by what I had said at the time, which was that I wouldn't be the one asking him out—the man makes the first move.

Though eventually I did end up asking him out.

It just took too long, and I wasn't waiting to have a *Shidduch*[3] anytime soon.

"Do you remember?"

The Amstel River was still glowing with the reflection of the sun. "That is not how the story goes," Nico said. "I knew I'd ask you out one day, from the moment we met."

I didn't remember this part, but this was how Nico put it: "At the office, I definitely noticed you, but was intimidated. People seemed to like you a lot. I wouldn't have dared to come up to you for a conversation. Usually someone else was already talking to you anyway."

It was true that my co-workers liked me and respected my opinions, which I never kept to myself. But I had been working at that firm for many years and knew all the ins and outs. People often came to me for help, or to have a chat. This social aspect was something I loved about my job. And, of course, my respectable position within the company.

For my twenty-fifth birthday, my colleagues wrote me a poem that said:

> *Congratulations to our sweetest star,*
> *Taller than all the men in the office by far,*
> *With a witty soul and a kind heart,*
> *Won't ever hold back her laughter at another's fart,*
> *She embroiders like a queen and plays tennis like a king,*
> *Now, who will be the lucky chap bringing her a ring?*
> *A bubbly gal our Hansje is, and oh so streetwise too,*
> *And stubborn like her brother, if the siblings only knew.*

The men at the office never flirted with me. They usually went for the shorter girls with fair hair, full lips, and higher cheekbones. Though they always included me in their group conversations, and I

---

3   *Shidduch* is a Jewish way of matchmaking.

often much preferred being on that side, rather than hanging at their smooth-talking lips.

I wasn't conventionally beautiful, and it wasn't something I ever minded. There was no man around who I wanted to look pretty for. Until Nico. With him, things were different. He was a respectful and decent man, not only when speaking to a girl he fancied. That honesty was one of the many things that attracted me to him.

"And the rest of your story isn't entirely true either," Nico claimed. "We didn't start dating after that day at the tennis court. It was a couple of months later in Autumn, when we went dancing on the weekends with Leo and Selma."

Even though I disagreed, there was no point in arguing about who was right or wrong. The only important thing was that we, fairly soon, got into a serious relationship, and a couple of years later, Nico proposed.

"We had so much fun together," I glistened nostalgically.

"Playing tennis, going camping or on a beach holiday to Scheveningen. Pubs, bike rides—"

"As long as you hadn't drunk too much the night before." I laughed.

"What do you mean?"

"Sorry to say, but you can't hold your liquor."

Nico got giggly after two glasses of wine. Maybe that's why we disagreed on who asked the other out first. He probably just couldn't remember. Though I kept that thought to myself.

"Before we knew it, I was wearing white and signing the *Ketubah*[4] in the Great Synagogue." Even though I mostly remembered the happy moments, I was still aware of the fact that on my wedding day, there had been a strange tension in the air. It had started in the morning, my family's dismay at the news on the radio stating the Vichy anti-Jewish legislation. "Luckily we're not getting married in France," I had jokingly said. Ab laughed but my parents did not respond. Since

---

4 *Ketubah* is a Jewish marriage contract.

that day, something had changed in my family. Something far greater than after the '30s crisis, when we lost most of our possessions. Even worse than the day we found out about my mother's illness.

My wedding day was the first moment I had witnessed my parents in complete despair. They were trying to hide it, of course, but I could tell by their looks and my mother's bitten off nails. It was supposed to be a celebration—my wedding day, for crying out loud!

"I still can't believe that we took that leap of faith," Nico said.

"What do you mean? By getting married?"

"Definitely. Especially when I remember all the threats that had been piling up since May that year."

Two days after our wedding, we heard on the news that, from November 7, Jews would have to leave non-Jewish associations and would be banned from bridge, dance, and tennis clubs. These were some of the most important activities to us growing up; they were the things that made us feel alive and young. And all this when our life as a married couple had only just begun.

"I wouldn't change it for the world," I said.

"Neither would I."

It was getting darker outside, and Nico looked at his wristwatch. "It's quite a long walk home. I think we should start heading back."

For a week, Nico and I had been walking the streets of Amsterdam without wearing our Yellow Stars. We would go far out of town, as it was best to avoid seeing anyone who could recognise us. Now we introduced ourselves as Theo and Pien Cornelissen. We didn't use those names very often, as we preferred to keep ourselves on the down low. Only in moments when it was necessary.

We arrived back in our neighbourhood. From a distance, I noticed a few police cars and people standing in the street. I stopped Nico.

"Is that our flat?"

A bunch of SS'ers and Dutch police officers walked out of our apartment building shaking their heads.

"We're not wearing our Yellow Stars," Nico worried.

We took a few steps back and made sure that no one saw us. Then we turned around and walked away. "Quickly, don't look back," I whispered.

"Hey!" A loud voice shouted. I wasn't sure whether it was directed at us. We continued walking whilst slowly snatching a look at the shouting man.

"You, there, stop!"

Nico and I started to run.

We were being followed. We ran faster, and so did they, their footsteps threading louder after each turn we made. My lungs were burning, and I had no clue where to go. I could hear Nico's breath getting louder. The sky was pitch black, and I couldn't tell how many men were following us, though their footsteps were drawing nearer and nearer. Our last turn was into a street which looked over the river. It was a dead end. Nico grabbed my arm and pulled me down behind a block of concrete. We could just about peek at the group of Gestapo officers, who weren't sure which street we had gone into. My gaze followed their torches, which illuminated the darkest corners. The only way out was by jumping in the river. Nico saw me glancing and shook his head.

"There must be another way," he whispered.

Their torches came closer. It would only take one moment of their light flashing onto us to catch us. One of the houses near us had a ladder which led to the roof. I pointed at it, and Nico didn't seem to like that idea either. The men distanced themselves by looking elsewhere. It was now or never.

I climbed the ladder first. Nico took off his glasses and immediately followed. The officers were shouting at one another. I was almost at the top of the ladder, near the roof, when one of the steps broke off and fell with a loud thud. Nico and I stood still for a moment and firmly held onto the ladder.

We made it up and could still see the officers in the distance, pointing their lights to the other side of the road. They were far enough not to notice us.

A loud voice in the distance asked, "Did you hear that?"

"*Klopfe an alle Türen*!" An SS'er shouted. They spread out and started bonking on all of the doors in the street, and their rowdy noises allowed us to quickly climb to the roof.

"Now what?" Nico asked. I shrugged my shoulders. We would have to stay on the roof until they all disappeared. "They might find the ladder." Nico was right. Besides, it was a gable roof, so there was nowhere for us to lay down and sleep. I looked down and felt my throat closing up. "Let's wait a little longer."

Nico rubbed my back. My eyes welled up with tears and I felt embarrassed. I wasn't crying because of sadness or frustration. I curled my hands into fists as I was burning up inside.

"Do you know how to get to Artis?" My voice was trembling with fear and anger.

Nico nodded. He stood up and noticed that the police were already five blocks away from us, heading in the wrong direction. We slowly got down the ladder. An old lady was sitting in front of her window. I stopped climbing down in shock. She stared me straight in the eyes, then put her finger to her lips and nodded with a smile. I nodded back and continued climbing down.

Once we left that area, we slowed our pace and tried to walk as unsuspiciously as possible.

———————

We arrived at the back door of the zoo. Nico knocked a few times, and a man opened the door ajar. We could only see his eyes, though I noticed the man was wearing a green hat.

"We're friends of Bert," Nico said.

The man sighed and was about to close the door. "We would love to see the monkeys!" Nico tried again.

He stopped for a moment.

"Boaz and Feline, they're our friends," I explained.

"And we would love to see the ... um ... the fish," Nico continued.

"Alright, alright. Get in."

He pulled us inside and closed the door. He gestured that we should stay quiet and follow him. His name tag said Peter. He led us through the zoo, to a small island with a giant rock, which was the monkey's abode. The island was surrounded by water. Peter slid a plank from our end, all the way to the island.

"Don't come out until I come tell you to," he said. We crossed over the plank to the other side. Inside the giant rock, there were a few other hiders. I recognised some of them from our neighbourhood.

My breath became less heavy, and I felt my heartbeat slow down a little.

Nico yawned. He put his arms around me and held onto my shoulder.

"We can't stay here forever."

Nico nodded.

"How are we going to tell Bonneka of our whereabouts?"

I had no idea.

For a couple of weeks, we had been pretending to be zookeepers by day, and hiding in the monkey rock or bear enclosure by night. Peter knew our names and had even sent out letters for us. One of them was to Bonneka, asking if there was any more news on whether we could go into hiding somewhere slightly safer. She had finally written back and given instructions.

So, on a warm evening in May, we left the zoo through the back door. It was still quite busy on the streets in Amsterdam, which was better for us, as it was more likely that we wouldn't draw any attention. I followed Nico, as he was the one with a better sense of orientation.

"It's better to leave Artis now, when it's still spring. Imagine staying in the open air in the middle of winter," I told him on our walk. He agreed. The zoo was a good place to hide temporarily, but we needed a long-term solution, as we didn't know how long we would have to hide for.

We eventually arrived at a tall, narrow townhouse along the canal in South Amsterdam. The house had a gorgeous brick-red facade and white auricular style ornaments, which framed the dual-pitched roof.

"Is this number eleven?"

We rang the doorbell twice so they would know it was us.

A blond maid opened the door. She greeted us both, as if we were guests, and let us inside. The maid introduced herself as Alex. We followed her through the corridor, into the hallway. The house was very big; it almost felt like being inside a mansion. In the hallway, there was a large, carpeted staircase, as well as a crystal chandelier hanging from the ceiling. The lights were dimmed, and Alex was holding a candle. She led us up the stairs to the second floor. We entered what I assumed was a study, and she told us to sit on the chairs and wait for the mistress of the house.

"Will you look at that," Nico pointed at a wide Edwardian bookcase. "The mistress must read a lot."

After a few minutes of waiting, Alex came into the room, behind her was a middle-aged woman in a night gown. She introduced herself as Michelle Nijsens but told us to call her Mrs. Nijsens. Apparently, she lived in the tall house by herself, with only her two maids, Alex and Shinta. They were both young women, probably around my age. Alex seemed slightly older than me, Hungarian, with only had a slight twang when speaking Dutch. Shinta was a slender girl with darker skin, sleek black hair, and unique facial features. I later found out that she was originally from Java.

Mrs. Nijsens explained to us that we would be hiding in the basement during most days. Alex or Shinta would make sure we would get food, water, and all things necessary. We would be hiding with a couple of others. If we wanted to leave the basement or go outside, we would have to tell one of the maids in advance, and they would provide me with a maid's uniform, or in Nico's case, with a boiler suit. But normally, we would not be allowed to leave the basement or even make a sound.

Once Mrs. Nijsens had left the room, Alex gave us two blankets. We followed her all the way to the basement. It was dark and chilly, and there was only one lightbulb hanging from the ceiling. Alex took us through the basement and unlocked a door with an iron padlock. Behind the door was, to our amazement, a room full of antique furniture, wooden boxes full of jewellery, artwork, and clocks.

Alex acknowledged the surprised looks on our faces. "This will distract the Germans when they come looking for you."

She lifted some wood on the floor and revealed a trapdoor, which opened to a hiding place. It was dark inside, but we could see a few others, laying down on a bed of straw, wrapped in blankets. Alex gave Nico a silver pocket lighter and whispered that he should only use it when necessary. We thanked her and lowered into the small space.

I thought about my baby, where she was, hoping she was safe. I knew it was best for a small child not to be trapped inside this small hiding place; it would do more harm than good. She was probably sleeping in a crib, inside a room with windows, with parents who were taking good care of her. That thought made me smile, even though I desperately wanted to hold her in my arms. Nico lay next to me, took my hand, and gently kissed it. We were both thinking the same thing.

That night, we held each other and cuddled ourselves to sleep.

The next morning, we were woken up by Shinta, who opened the trapdoor to give us our breakfast. We could finally stand and stretch our legs.

There were three others hiding with us: a little girl, her father, and a teenage boy.

Shinta put a platter on the antique table. There was bread, cheese, and orange juice. "The Spaniards have blessed the country with three-hundred tons of oranges," she said. There were only four chairs, so the man let his daughter sit, whilst he ate his food standing. Shinta told us she would let us eat and come back later to clean up.

"Mrs. Nijsens seems to be a tough one." I tried to make conversation.

"You'll learn to appreciate her," the man replied, devouring his piece of bread. He gave his cheese to the little girl.

"Eat up! You still need to grow, Ilona."

The man introduced himself as Remco. He was a tall blond man, probably in his mid-thirties.

"My name is Hanna, and this is my husband, Nathan."

"But you can call me Nico."

They shook hands.

"Aren't we supposed to stay quiet?" I asked.

"Not when they allow us out. It's probably only six in the morning now," the teenage boy responded. "I'm Gabriel. Nice to meet you." The boy had a charming smile. I was sure he must have a lot of success with girls his age. But he also seemed quite shy.

Shinta came back down in a hurry. She opened the trapdoor. "Get inside now!"

We rushed inside the little space, and she closed it behind us. I could hear the sounds she was making, taking the tray with the food and locking the door behind her.

We spent what felt like an hour trapped inside the small space, not moving or making a sound. At some point, Ilona had to sneeze, and Remco put his hand in front of her mouth and shushed the little girl.

We could hear the sound of the chain on the door rattling. The door was opened, and there were footsteps, trying to tread quietly. I held my breath for as long as I could, until someone opened the trapdoor. I felt a sharp acceleration of my heartbeat, until I saw who it was.

"Congratulations, you passed the test."

It was Mrs. Nijsens. My face turned red.

I had been thinking about all the things that could have gone wrong.

"You'll thank me for it," she said.

I didn't want to say anything, for I knew that she had full control over what could happen to us. Yet, I realised, she would not deliberately do anything to hurt us. She was in a similar vulnerable position. I wondered why she was doing this, why she was helping us.

After a couple of weeks of living inside the basement, not being able to track the intangible passing of time, Alex came down one day (or night, I wasn't sure). She opened the trapdoor and took Ilona out. By that time, I had found out that Alex and Remco were a couple, and that Ilona was their illegitimate daughter.

I realised this when Alex had once come down to give us our supper.

Ilona started speaking to her in Hungarian, which surprised me.

Gabriel was a quiet boy, who usually seemed to be quite lost in his own world.

Later, when Nico had gone to the other side of the basement, to do his needs, I started speaking to Remco.

"I'm not a Jew, just a journalist," he told me. "But Ilona is, through her mother. Alex comes from a family of bankers in Budapest. Her family told her and her sisters to flee the country as they suspected a certain decay of events. Fortunately, she managed to enter the Netherlands in the late thirties, assuming the liberal city of Amsterdam would keep its neutrality during the war. But when she arrived, things were already worse than she imagined, even though the local Jews kept positive about the situation."

What Remco was saying reminded me of my life in the 1930s. I had never expected events to turn out this way.

"How did you two meet?" I asked.

He smiled, seemingly reminiscing. "Being a journalist for many years, you tend to meet interesting people from all sorts of backgrounds. I was writing a controversial report about the uprise of the NSDAP and its allies. Alex was one of my informants for this piece. We fell in love, and with an incidental miracle, our little Ilona was born."

Alex came from a wealthy family; it reminded me of how I had been living before the crisis. Big banquets for charity events, a future full of opportunities, luxurious clothes, and we even had maids of our own. Still, I never experienced a feeling of despair, even after we lost all of that. It was easier to think of all the exciting things ahead, like starting a life of my own. All this hiding was much worse.

Alex had taken Ilona upstairs to go for a walk. The little girl had blond hair, so it would be unlikely for anyone to suspect them of being Jewish.

"Luckily, Alex found Mrs. Nijsens, who also has her beef with the Nazis," Remco started to clarify things for me. I wanted to know more, but before I could ask, Alex and Ilona had come back from their walk. Alex asked us to go back inside the trapdoor for a few hours.

"Don't worry, Mrs. Nijsens has planned something fun for you all some night this week. At least there's something to look forward to," she said before closing the trapdoor.

Days went by where we rarely saw the sunlight. I went out once a week, usually accompanied by Alex or Shinta. One morning, when I was allowed to go out, I gave Nico our good luck kiss, before putting on my maid's uniform and leaving the house. Shinta and I were going to the market. By now, it was already mid-July, even though the weather was still quite chilly. Summer had always been my favourite season, which was why I missed the beaches in Scheveningen, and why I always appreciated houses where a lot of natural light came through. The dark basement made me miss the sunlight even more.

Shinta and I were walking along the Amstel River, closer to the centre of the city. We passed by the diamond district, which was where father used to work before the economic crisis. When we were kids, Ab and I used to roam these streets after school, visiting father at his shop or playing with the other kids of parents who worked in the district. I knew many who had lived there or used to have diamond cutting shops in the area, including that guy from the Jewish Council, Asscher. Even though I felt a slight resentment thinking about the man, I couldn't help but understand his reasonings. I used to know his children; they were close to my age. The family had done so much good, my father Mozes used to say. They even gave shelter to Belgian refugees during the Great War. He probably thought he was doing what was best for his family, to our community's detriment.

We continued along the river, and I was deeply buried in my thoughts. Every inch of the city reminded me of my past life in Amsterdam. It made me think of the places Betty hadn't yet seen, and the ones I desperately wanted to show her.

"How did you meet your husband?" Shinta asked.

"It's an arguable topic," I replied, still in my train of thought. "My mother used to love going to the Albert Cuyp market," I said. "Mrs. Nijsens actually reminds me of her."

"Your mother must have been a fierce woman then."

"Have you known her long?"

"Since before I could walk."

It surprised me, and I was curious to know more about Shinta. She was a well-spoken and naturally charming girl, in a sort of modest, yet sincere manner.

"Your Dutch is impeccable."

She grinned. "I would hope so. It's the only language I know."

"Did Mrs. Nijsens take you in when you were a child?"

"I'm her husband's bastard," she told me bluntly.

We arrived at the market. It was a Saturday, which meant there were a lot of people, even though food was getting more and more scarce. When I had been a child, a third of the market stalls were owned by people from our community. Now the stall owners seemingly wouldn't have to fight about which stall they could get, even though there was less to sell anyway. We had come very early, but still had to stand in a long cue.

"I hope they'll have some things left," Shinta was anxiously looked around.

I thought about what she had told me before. Now that there were more people around, it wasn't wise to ask personal questions; regardless of that, I was curious to know more. When it was our turn to go to one of the stands, I let Shinta do most of the talking. Whenever they would ask me something, I would change my accent to make it sound slightly South European, hoping people wouldn't suspect me of being a Dutch woman in hiding.

"Potatoes, sauerkraut, turnips, pears, green beans . . . I'm happy we came early, we even got some mussels!"

We started heading back on the Rijnstraat, which was close to where our family had lived before we were forced to move out. Our flat was on a side street. I didn't tell Shinta that we were close to my old home, as I was hoping that we could pass by that place, in the Lekstraat. When we came close to the intersection, we heard some loud noises. We stopped, not knowing where the sounds were coming from. It couldn't be thunder, as the sun was still shining through the clouds. People around us started shouting and running inside their homes. An older lady opened her door shouted to us. "Girls! Quickly come inside!"

Shinta grabbed my arm and dragged me with her, inside the lady's house. We entered and threw ourselves on the floor, putting our hands on our heads. I lay still, not knowing what was happening. We could only hear a few loud noises, but they sounded too far away. Before we knew it, the sounds had stopped, and it was as if nothing had happened.

The old lady was struggling to get up. I took her hands and helped her get into an armchair. "Perhaps they are trying to scare us," the lady said.

"We should stay here for a couple more minutes." Shinta thanked the lady for letting us inside. We had taken the food bags inside with us, but had dropped them on the floor, and the potatoes and pears were everywhere. I went to pick them back up and gave a few pears to the lady.

"Where are you from?" she asked us kindly.

"I'm from the Dutch Indies[5], and my friend is Portuguese."

The house was small, and it seemed as though the lady was living by herself. There were no pictures of any children or grandchildren. She tried to keep us inside by chatting, but Shinta told her we had to leave. We thanked her again and left the house.

"Kind lady. Lonely, I suppose," I said.

"But we can't keep her company. Nowadays, you can't trust anyone. Let's hurry back before she calls the police."

I didn't suspect the older woman of thinking I would be a Jew or let alone calling the police on me. But I knew Shinta was right that we couldn't take any chances. We walked along the Rijnstraat, and I could see the Lekstraat in the corner of my eye. "What do you think happened?" I asked with a slight concern. Shinta shook her head, unknowingly.

We had long passed the Lekstraat when I suddenly stopped in shock. There was a guy, walking towards us. I rapidly turned the other way and started speed walking in the other direction. "What's wrong?" Shinta followed me, quickening her pace.

"We need to go," I whispered. "Now."

I tried to steady my breath but felt my chest pounding. We entered different streets, until he was finally out of sight.

"I know that guy," I told Shinta, who seemed worried.

---

5   **The Dutch Indies** is the colony of what is now modern-day Indonesia.

"How?" She asked, "Who is he?"

"I'm not sure, but I have seen him before." On our way back, I tried to remember where I knew him from.

"He didn't notice or look at us in any off-putting way, so maybe he didn't recognise you."

She could be right. I wasn't even sure who he was, but I was certain of having seen his face before. He was a tall, well-built man, with a ginger, full, and scruffy beard.

When we got back to the house, I put the grocery bag on the table and went to the basement to see Nico. "Thank God you're alright!" He hugged me tightly and caressed my back.

I asked if he knew what had happened.

"The Americans dropped bombs on North Amsterdam."

I couldn't believe it. "Are you sure it's not German propaganda?"

"The airplanes were Flying Fortresses, American heavy bombers," Gabriel said. I was surprised to hear his voice. "I used to have a small B-17 model, always wanted to be a pilot." That explained his knowledge of the aircraft.

"Why would they bomb Amsterdam?" I asked worryingly. "Oh god! Betty!"

I felt a sharp twinge in my chest. Nico tried to calm me down. I wanted to cry. We didn't have any way of knowing if Betty was unsafe or hurt.

"Hansje, we don't know anything for sure. There might not even be any victims. Don't put these images inside your head." Nico tried to be helpful, but it just made me more upset.

"How can you say that? She's your child, too, but I seem to be the only one who cares!" I regretted those words the moment they slipped out of my mouth.

"Don't push me away," he said, trying to hide that I had offended him. I sat down and buried my face in my hands. Remco was holding Ilona tightly, gently reassuring her that everything was alright.

Alex came downstairs.

"They hit a few churches and residential areas, mostly the Vogel and Van Der Pek neighbourhoods," she seemed troubled.

I wasn't exactly sure where Betty was hidden, though I was almost certain that it wasn't in any of those areas. I felt shame for what I had said to Nico. Other children and families must have gotten hurt from the attack. At least I was almost certain that Betty was alright, but it didn't change the fact that many others were probably suffering. I held my pride, stood up, and apologised to Nico, who still seemed upset by my remark.

"At least we know she's alright," he said, trying to shake off his chagrin.

"But other children aren't. We need to do something!" I turned to Alex and Remco.

"We can't," he said. "Unless you want to be sent away."

I knew he was right, but it did not minimise my urge to act. Mrs. Nijsens came downstairs. She instructed Alex to go back up and help Shinta prepare supper.

"Now that the Germans have something else on their minds, we can enjoy a nice family meal together," Mrs. Nijsens said. "Alex will let you know when dinner's ready."

Before Mrs. Nijsens could leave, I got angry. "Are we going to ignore the whole situation and celebrate?"

She turned around and looked me straight in the eyes. "I suppose you can stay in the basement if you prefer." I couldn't find a response, and before I knew it, she was gone.

"You can't carry the world on your shoulders," Remco said.

I regretted my words to Mrs. Nijsens, but still felt tense about the whole situation. I had provoked Mrs. Nijsens and hurt Nico. I knew I had to redeem myself, but also didn't entirely want to. I stood strongly by what I thought, even though I knew that a nice social supper in the dinning room would do me some good, physically and mentally.

Remco let go of Ilona, and she approached me slowly.

"I think you are very brave," she said. It made me smile.

I crouched down to her eye level. "Thank you, Ilona. So are you."

Her words gave me a small boost of hope.

SUMMER, 1943

MRS. NIJSENS STILL WASN'T FOND of me. I had tried many things to make her like me, but they all seemed to fail, and she kept her distance.

However, Mrs. Nijsens did have a strong appreciation towards Nico, and really enjoyed his company. They had a similar kind of intellectual humour.

Some evenings, she would find an excuse to ask one of us to come upstairs. It was mostly to fix things, or to help her with certain administrative letters. I assumed it was to have some company, too, as it must have been difficult to live in that big house with only her two maids.

She often asked Nico upstairs, which secretly made me quite jealous. I knew the guy couldn't fix a sink, even if he put his mind to it. I guess I should have been happier for him, as it was probably nice to get out of the basement for a change. We spent a lot of time crouched in the small space underneath the trapdoor, and during the high summer months, the basement became stuffier. There wasn't a lot of air in that room. So, it was always nice to be out every once in a while.

One evening, Mrs. Nijsens sent Alex to come pick me up. I followed her up the stairs, wondering why Mrs. Nijsens wanted to see me. All the curtains in the house were closed. Alex led me into the living room where she told me to wait, then she went back downstairs, I assumed to see Ilona and Remco.

The living room was almost as big as our whole apartment at the Lekstraat. Next to the window, in between two bookcases, there was a mahogany grand piano. I approached, to have a closer look. It was a Steinway & Sons. *It must be extremely expensive*, I thought. The keyboard was covered and seemed to be almost untouched.

Mrs. Nijsens entered the living room with Shinta behind her, who was carrying a tray with a teapot and Dété, a tea surrogate. She put down the tray and added the Dété tablets to the teapot.

"You may take the rest of the night off," Mrs. Nijsens said to Shinta, who nodded and left the room.

Mrs. Nijsens poured the tea and offered me a cup.

"Your husband told me you're a fine pianist," she said, sipping her cup. "Play me something."

She saw my uncertainty and reassured me. "No one is going to enter this house just because of the piano's music."

"It's not that," I had to admit. "It's just been a very long time since I've played."

"I've been told it's like riding a bike." She seemed eager, so I put down my teacup and lifted the fall board. The first song that my fingers remembered was "Spring," from Vivaldi's Four Seasons. I started playing and heard how its tuning seemed close to perfect, which confirmed that this piano hadn't been used often, even though the model was a couple of decades old.

When I turned around to look at Mrs. Nijsens, I could see that her eyes were closed, and she was slowly swaying to the song.

The song almost finished, and she approached the piano, stroking its smooth rim.

"My husband used to play this song," she said wistfully.

"I didn't know you were married," I lied. There were no pictures in the house, which made it easy to assume that she had no family.

"Shinta told me you know," Mrs. Nijsens confessed. "It's no secret." She put her hand on the inside of the rim and took out a picture. It was of her, when she was younger, and a man. Handsome, wearing small, round glasses, he almost reminded me of Nico.

"Where is he?" I probably shouldn't have asked, but Mrs. Nijsens didn't seem to mind.

"You can't imagine what it's like not knowing."

I wasn't sure what she meant and didn't dare to ask further. "Because of Shinta, you must think he doesn't love me. It isn't true. We loved each other dearly. I just couldn't give him a family. And besides, most men go off the rails. Their desires are different than ours."

I firmly disagreed with her statement. "Nico wouldn't."

"You don't know that."

She hadn't answered my question. "So, you don't know where he is?"

"Last thing I heard was that the Japanese put him in a work camp."

"What was he doing in Southeast Asia?"

"Olivier is a diplomat."

Was a diplomat, I thought.

"I can imagine."

"Can imagine what?" Mrs. Nijsens poured more tea and took a loud sip. "What it's like, when a person dear to you is far away. When you don't know where they are or whether you will ever see them again."

Mrs. Nijsens pointed out that it was different, because at least Nico and I were together.

"I'm not talking about Nico." I turned to face the keyboard and started playing Für Elise.

The images were flashing through my mind. Of Betty, sitting down next to me and miming that she was the one playing the song, tapping each of her small fingers on the imaginary floor piano. Swinging her head from one side to the other. Betty loved this song.

The doorbell rang, followed by three loud knocks.

From Mrs. Nijsen's expression, I could see that she was not expecting company. There was no time to go back to the basement, so she gestured that I should hide inside the utility closet. I tiptoed inside the closet and was a bit too tall, so I had to crouch down behind the door space. Mrs. Nijsens closed and locked the closet behind me. I could hear footsteps hurrying down the stairs and was assuming it was Shinta running towards the front door. The sounds were muffled, but I could catch a couple of things that were said. Shinta introduced herself as the maid, and a man's voice was speaking in Dutch. The voices were too far away to make out what was being said. Then I heard another voice asking about "Frau Nijsens." Two men were at the door, I thought, a Dutchman and a German. I felt paralysed, trying to calm my breath and not make a sound. The first memory that came into my mind was when we had been hiding inside the basement and had heard those footsteps. It had all been a test, to see how still and quiet we could be. This couldn't be a test, I thought. Secretly, I hoped it was.

Shinta was trying to keep the men outside, as I heard her panicking when they unwelcomely entered the house.

"Mrs. Nijsens, how are you this evening?" The Dutch man sounded quite harmless, but then again, most collaborators did.

"What can I do for you gentlemen this evening?" From what I could hear, it sounded as if she was pretending to be intoxicated.

"We got an anonymous tip that there have been some strange things happening here. Do you mind if we take a look?"

She knew they were just asking to be polite and would search the premises regardless. "Well, let me know if you find my husband. I have been wondering where he's been hiding, Joeri," she said bluntly. So, she knew this man.

"It's Mr. Molenaar to you," he spat. "Yes, the situation is unfortunate, but we've been doing our best to try and get Mr. Nijsens back."

"That's a load of *lulkoek*[6]."

The German man seemed to be getting agitated with Mr. Molenaar, even though I didn't understand most of what he said. I could understand a few words, like *"Sie ist betrunken,"* she's drunk, or *"Wir kommen morgen mit den anderen,"* that they would come back tomorrow, and I assumed they'd be bringing a few other police or SS officers.

Why were they coming this late anyway? Perhaps they wanted to have a look before we could escape. But then why would they come back tomorrow? Mr. Molenaar and Mrs. Nijsens spent a couple more minutes discussing her husband. He translated everything to his German colleague, who laughed and called her a *"geile witwe."* Mrs. Nijsens pretended not to know what he meant, but she knew damn well that he had called her a horny widow.

"Your husband is a well-respected man, Mrs. Nijsens. Perhaps you should tone down the drinking and remember to keep your manners. You wouldn't want to ruin his reputation, would you?"

"You are completely right, Mr. Molenaar. I feel ashamed and, frankly, quite foolish. You won't be hearing about any strange behaviours in my house again. I'm just lonely sometimes." Her words sounded sincere, yet I couldn't imagine Mrs. Nijsens saying these things truthfully.

"That is enough, now," Mr. Molenaar interrupted her and translated it to the German officer. "Don't do anything you will regret. Good evening, ma'am."

They both left.

---

6 ***Lulkoek*** is a vulgar Dutch saying that literally means "a cake of nonsense."

Shinta closed the front door, but I had to wait inside the closet for a few more minutes, just to make sure they wouldn't come back. After a while, she finally opened the closet and let me out. Mrs. Nijsens was sitting at the kitchen table.

"Let that be a lesson," she avoided looking me in the eyes. "Us women have to pretend to obey. When you act like a wreck, they want to teach us how to behave, and it makes them feel manly."

"That was quite a good act you put on there."

"Sometimes our safety is more important than our dignity." Those words struck hard.

I had always been surrounded by strong women, who didn't let down their guard, and men, who respected us women. Needless to say, I knew many women for whom this was not the case. However, in my household, Ab and I had always been treated equally, and he never spoke to me differently just because I was a woman.

When I first met her, Mrs. Nijsens struck me as a tough and brave woman. She was reserved, but it seemed like a way to protect herself. Now she had made a complete fool of herself in front of those officers—for her own protection, as well as ours.

"But they might come back," I worried.

"Not anytime soon. Don't worry. The only thing they're suspecting me of is adultery, not keeping you all in hiding."

She finally looked me in the eyes, and I could faintly see that her eyes were red and that she had even maybe been shedding a few tears.

"You're very lucky," she said with a warm smile. I hadn't ever seen her smile like that before, which took me by surprise. And I also wasn't sure what she meant.

"Your husband," she explained. "He loves and respects you a lot. It isn't something you often encounter."

It made me feel fortunate, knowing that Nico had been speaking highly of me. Not something I expected of him, as he was usually reserved and kept his thoughts to himself. "I haven't thanked you yet," I said. "For letting us stay here. I can't imagine what you must be risking."

"Something beyond your ken," she replied neutrally. She wrapped a few chocolate chunks into a linen cloth and asked me to bring it down for the others. Shinta led me back to the basement and opened the trapdoor.

I lay down next to Nico and kissed his lips. "Are you awake?" I whispered. He answered something, half asleep. I gave him a piece of chocolate. He murmured something, nibbled on the chocolate, and fell asleep again.

That night, I couldn't sleep. I just thought about Ab, about father, and about Betty. I missed them so. Luckily, I had Nico sleeping next to me, for which I was incredibly grateful. But besides that, I was plagued by guilt and sorrow. Betty and Ab were safe, I thought, even though I couldn't know for sure. But of father's whereabouts, I didn't have a clue. He was probably somewhere foreign, outside of the Netherlands. Perhaps they sent him off East to work, but he had been so weak the last few times I had seen him. I couldn't imagine him being fit for manual labour.

I thought back on what Mrs. Nijsens had told me. "Sometimes our safety is more important than our dignity."

So far, the occupiers had taken almost everything away from me. My house, my freedom, my family, my daughter . . . But there was one thing they hadn't taken yet, which was my dignity. I wondered how long it would take until they would get a hold of that too.

AUTUMN, 1943—PART I

THERE WERE SOUNDS coming from upstairs, furniture being pushed around. Most of the noise was muffled, but we held our breath to listen for signs of what was happening. Dozens of German officers were searching the house for clues. I was trying to put my mind at ease; after all, it could have just been a regular house search, and we were well hidden.

Now there were just four of us: Remco, Ilona, Nico, and me.

Two days prior, Gabriel had left Mrs. Nijsens house, as he had been planning on fleeing the country to go to Portugal. From there on, he would take a boat to the United States of America. I found out that Gabriel's parents had been sent away a long time ago. But before being caught, they paid a lot of money to ensure that Gabriel would be safe. First, he had to hide in Mrs. Nijsens house, until an organisation would come to pick him up in the middle of the night to lead him on an escape route to Spain.

I thought he might have been caught and questioned as to where he had been hidden. It seemed highly unlikely that Gabriel would have told them anything about our whereabouts, but then again, who was I to know that for sure.

It turned out I was wrong. Gabriel had escaped the Nazis and was, hopefully, already on his way to freedom. But something, or someone, else had given away our location.

Ilona was firmly holding onto her father, telling him that she was scared. Remco shushed her. This wasn't a test—that we knew for sure. The Germans were shouting and throwing around everything upstairs. They loudly slammed the basement door open and hastened down the stairs.

"*Öffne diese Tür!*" one of the Germans shouted, shaking the iron pad lock. Someone must have obeyed. I could hear the door opening and a heap of footsteps entering the antique room.

Nico took my hand and squeezed it firmly. I felt a cramp in my leg, but I kept it in its position, not wanting to make a sound. Again, my heart was pounding, but now even more than it ever had. It was so loud, I could hear the pulse beating in my ears. I got frightened after a few loud stomps on the ground, just above us, and tried not to make a sound. Nico squeezed me tighter, as if communicating to me that everything would be alright.

"*Sie sind hier, ich kann es riechen.*" The SS officers were just above us. It was as if the man was standing less than two meters away from me.

The carpet was removed, and before I knew it, they opened the trapdoor. "*Der Hauptgewinn!*" one of them shouted. One of the soldiers grabbed Ilona. Remco was trying to hold on to her, but they took her out of his grip. She shouted and cried. Alex was tightly held by one of the soldiers, and she was screaming in Hungarian, probably trying to tell Ilona that everything was going to be alright. One of the other soldiers grabbed my arm and forcefully lifted me up. I tried to resist for a few seconds but realised that it was pointless. There were too many of them, and they were too strong for us to escape. Two officers were holding Mrs. Nijsens, emitting hopelessness and defeat. I recognised one of the men from somewhere. I tried hard to think back on where I had seen that man before.

Then I remembered.

How could I have forgotten that red beard? It was one of Klaas' friends, who had been there that day when he had scolded me. And in July, I had seen him again, during the German bomb attack on North Amsterdam.

The man wasn't dressed as an officer, but he seemed particularly pleased about this whole situation.

"Well done, Mr. Molenaar." An officer shook his hand. So, this was the infamous Joeri Molenaar. I couldn't help but feel as if I had been stabbed in my chest. Was this whole arrest my fault? Or was it the result of a sequence of events which had instigated suspicion? I wasn't sure, but what I did know was that we had been caught. Mr. Molenaar gave me a dirty look of disdain, which shook my core. I had been looked down upon and unpleasantly stared at over the last couple of years— but this look was one of pure hatred, which I would never forget.

"There's someone missing!" Mr. Molenaar was still keeping his eyes on me. How could he have known that Gabriel had been hiding with us?

"This woman has a child," he said. My whole body paralysed. "Where is it?"

I felt my insides burning when he called her *it*.

"We don't know, and neither will you!" Nico's voice shrilled. The officer punched Nico's stomach. My instincts wanted me to yell something, but I didn't dare to move or say anything else. They dragged all of us upstairs and took us outside. Remco, Ilona, Alex, Shinta, Mrs. Nijsens, Nico, and me.

We were taken outside and shoved inside a utility truck. I was cramped next to Mrs. Nijsens, whose face was paler than I had ever seen it. I took her hand.

"Safety over dignity, Mrs. Nijsens," I said.

She turned to look at me, and with a soft tone, she said, "Call me Michelle."

We arrived at the police station and got out of the cramped utility truck. Shinta was nowhere to be seen, and in a way, I hoped that she escaped the Nazis. Perhaps she would find a way to contact Mrs. Nijsens' husband, and maybe he could get her out of this mess. The officers forcefully took us inside, but left Remco, Ilona, and Alex in the truck. I overheard them saying they wanted to make our interrogation as quick as possible.

"In and out." The man clicked his finger.

We got separated and were taken to different interrogation rooms. It was a small space, with pale walls and four chairs bolted to the floor, no table. The windowless room was cold and brightly lit.

I was trying not to show panic, even though I felt I had done nothing wrong. It was a strange feeling, being trapped inside that small room, like a prisoner who hadn't committed any moral crimes. Two men entered. One was a tall and chubby SS officer, who reminded me a little bit of Hendrick Colijn, who had been the Dutch Prime Minister twice. I never liked that man, and it gave me a bad feeling about his SS lookalike.

The other man was Mr. Molenaar. He was clean shaven, unlike the last time I had seen him.

"Get up," the SS officer said aggressively. This was not going to be a civil interrogation.

My legs still hurt from having been crammed inside that basement's little space for so long. *It's probably better if I stand up*, I told myself. I didn't want to let those men have full control over me, even though the ball was now in their court. *What would Ab do?* I thought. Probably outsmart them.

Mr. Molenaar was translating for the SS officer.

"You are going to be sentenced for the crimes you have committed and sent to a prison in Drenthe."

"Am I not getting a trial?" I asked.

The SS officer, who didn't even understand what I said, hit my cheek with his flat hand. It was so quick that I didn't even realise the man had struck me until after it had happened. Even though it didn't hurt a lot, the gesture shocked me, and I felt denigrated. This wasn't going to be a fair trial, that I felt sure of. They wouldn't even care about anything I had to say. All they wanted to get out of me was some sort of confession and answers to their questions. I would rather hang than rat out a single soul to those bastards.

"Don't try to outsmart us. It won't work." Mr. Molenaar didn't seem even slightly shocked about the slap. "We just want to help you." His tone was more human, but mendacious.

A woman entered the interrogation room, wearing a grey suit with a knee-length pleated skirt, her blond hair tied up in a lower bun with a beret that was slightly too high up.

She faked a smile. I could have seen that from miles away. Mr. Molenaar and the SS officer stood by the door, trying not to interfere.

The woman shook my hand and told me to sit down. I obeyed, and she sat opposite me.

Stand up, sit down, these people had to make up their minds.

"Mrs. Mullem, correct? Can I call you Hanna?"

I wanted to tell her to call me Mrs. Mullem, but I knew I had to act friendly with this woman, pretend that I was fooled by her sincerity, though I more than well realised the disingenuous character she was playing.

"You can call me Tina. And I am a mother," she claimed far too quickly. "Two beautiful sons, one of them only fourteen months old. You and I are alike. We are both hard workers, who would do anything to keep our children happy and safe."

She didn't know a single thing about me.

"It pains me to know that you are separated from your beautiful baby—"

"Boy," I responded.

"I could sense that you and I shared that. Nurturing the men of the future," Tina continued. "It hurt me when I heard that your son was separated from his mother, which is why I asked the chief if I could speak to you."

She handed me a photograph of a floor plan. "This is a place in Drenthe, where your family and friends are staying too. We want to keep your community as safe as possible, and to be able to do this, we must send you to Westerbork. It is a place where you shall be able to practice your religious duties, as well as work and enjoy leisurely activities, without the fear of being judged by those around you."

She explained that, seeing our situation of being found in hiding, we would be sent to the village's prison. But that if I were to arrive there with a child, they would definitely make an exception for us.

"Lieutenant Gemmeker, the current commander of Westerbork, is a decent man with good morals. And I can only imagine how desperately you would want to be reunited with your son."

"Thank you for your kind words of comfort. Being reunited with my son does sound like something I wouldn't think twice about," I lied. "Unfortunately, I have no idea where he is."

The corners of her mouth dropped.

"Do you have a name? I'm sure we can find him for you."

"My son's name?"

"The name of the person he's with." Tina didn't realise I was playing dumb.

"I don't know."

"You gave your only son to a complete stranger?" her face darkened. She said something in German to the SS officer near the door. He shrugged his shoulders.

Tina swiftly stood up and ordered me to do the same. The officer approached, and without hesitation, he punched me right in the stomach. This time, it hurt a lot, and I tried not to collapse onto the floor. She uttered something else, but I was too focused on trying to catch my breath.

"Where is your son?" she repeated, more loudly this time.

"I don't have a son," I said, gasping for air.

This angered her more, and she pulled my hair back and punched me in the face. I could feel the copper taste of blood in my mouth. The shame and injustice hurt more than the physical pain they inflicted. And still, it was worth it. As long as Betty was safe, I was the one in control—not them.

The next day, they dropped us off at the Hollandsche Schouwburg, located in the heart of the Jewish neighbourhood in Amsterdam. Across the street, we could a see bunch of little children, toddlers, and even babies gathered on the pavement in front of a kindergarten.

One little girl, who couldn't have been older than three, was drawing some flowers with chalk on the pavement. She had olive skin and squinted eyes, which reminded me of Betty. The girl looked at me and giggled, trying to show off her beautiful drawing. I smiled back, and Nico noticed.

"Just like our little one," he said regretfully. The SS had beaten Nico up too. His wounds seemed even more severe than my own. And they had even broken his glasses.

Surrounded by dozens of other families, youngsters, and elderly, we had to enter the Hollandse Schouwburg and wait. The Schouwburg had been a theatre before, and a couple of years prior, only Jews had been allowed to play there or attend the performances. The moment we entered the building, I sensed a whole new feeling of lethargy. The theatre, which we had once known as a place of joy and artistic freedom, was now completely destroyed. The stage was bare, stripped of its decoration and charm. Its artwork, paintings, and statues, which had previously graced the halls, were nowhere to be seen. The seats had been ripped from the floor and placed against the walls. But worst of all was the gloomy and scary feeling from all those who were there. All the lights were out, completely darkening the space. Everyone was crammed together, terrified, surrounded by SS soldiers strutting around the building.

They pushed us towards a side of the building which was supposed to be the prisoner's area. Nico and I sat down against one of the walls, and I squeezed his hand.

"Where to next in our adventure?" I asked ironically.

A shadow stood up from the crowd and walked towards us. The shadow came closer, revealing that it was a woman, and I was trying to recall where I had seen her before.

"Feline." Nico recognised her.

She hugged us both and sat down. It was so dark that we could barely see her. I wondered whether she looked happy to see us or if she had been crying out of frustration. Her voice revealed that it was a combination of both.

"How did they find you?" Even though there were a few murmurs from other people around us, I tried to stay quiet and make ourselves unnoticeable to the officers.

"Someone on the street suspected me and reported it to the authorities. Luckily, they didn't catch me in Artis, so I could lie about where I had been hiding. Everyone else there, including Boaz, are safe."

"Thank God," I said. "We got betrayed too."

"It's because those stingy Dutch are earning guilders for every Jew they report," Feline said angrily.

This shocked me. That was why there was so many people in the Schouwburg, and why they were still bringing in more. The whole city had been participating in a Jew hunt, almost as if it were a game to them.

"How's your little one?" Feline asked.

"Safe."

Time went by so slowly, and we only received a very limited amount of food. We must have only been there a couple of days when the SS general pointed at our section in the room and told us to follow them. Some people got upset, complaining that they had been waiting there for almost a week and wanted to leave too. But the more they complained, the more aggressive the officers became.

Nico, Feline, and I just listened to what the man said and followed him into the corridor. I could hear screams behind me but was trying to distract myself from the sounds. I didn't want to think about the officers hitting the scared and weak, but it was an image I could not get out of my mind.

"Most important rule: never talk directly to the SS or NSB," Feline warned me.

We walked through the corridor, to the front desk to register. It was a big, organised mess. Most of this was happening in the dark of the night, and I couldn't help but wonder how long it would take until people became aware of what was happening to us. The Gestapo could do anything or take us anywhere they wanted, and no one would make a sound. Now I understood why so many people had been disappearing into thin air.

Maybe even my father, Mozes, had gone through the Hollandse Schouwburg. I wondered what he would've thought about the destruction of the building we used to love. And in a way, it also scared me; his weakness couldn't survive all of this. The hours, days, or even weeks of waiting, the scarce food and water. We hadn't even been allowed to go to the bathroom, and had to do our needs in a bucket in the middle of a hall. I hadn't lived the last few years as luxuriously as when I was a child, but this whole situation was a disgraceful nightmare. My hair was greasy and unwashed. Its smell made me feel grim. Before, I never had a problem with getting my hands dirty, but the more the Gestapo tried to undermine me, the cleaner I wanted to look. To prove them wrong. They would be obliged to see me as a civilised human being and not a filthy thing they wanted to send away and get rid of.

When we finished registering, they took us outside.

In a way, I wasn't sure whether I was lucky to leave the Schouwburg. Where were they taking us?

———————

The Central Station in Amsterdam was quieter and darker than the last time I was there. It was where I used to take the train to go on holidays.

I was reminded of my first beach holiday with Nico, proud to finally call him my boyfriend. I imagined myself holding a suitcase, with Nico's hand in mine. Pien, Henry, Lientje, Beb, Selma, Leo, and Frank were with us. Selma ran around trying to find the right platform.

"Calm down," Leo said, "The train is only in half an hour." Nico reminded me that I had to write a letter to father when we'd arrive. My suitcase was fully packed with summer wear and a few jumpers for the evenings when it would get colder. The girls and I had gone shopping two days earlier to buy ourselves swimwear. Pien and Selma helped me find the perfect bathing suit: a honey coloured with a low dipped back.

"It's way too revealing," I had said embarrassedly, but the girls thought it was the perfect fit. Pien reminded me that the halter neck still kept it modest, whilst Selma emphasised that the one-piece made my long legs stand out and that the colour suited my olive skin.

Eventually, I didn't end up getting that one. I bought another bathing suit: a navy-blue maillot with a closed back and a lined top.

"If we get married, I'll buy the yellow one to spice things up." I laughed with my girlfriends.

Now, all those worries felt foolish. It didn't matter whether a bathing suit was yellow or blue, or if the back was too revealing. Nico was still holding my hand; that part hadn't changed. But we weren't surrounded by our friends anymore. Now we were waiting, demeaned by SS officers who saw us as lawbreakers. The ones who hadn't obeyed the rules, the ones who had been in hiding. In a way, I felt proud about having been able to defy the law this way, as it was our only way to bite back.

The train's journey could have been an hour or five; I wasn't sure. The further away from Amsterdam we got, the emptier the landscape became. Mostly meadows and fields. I had never been to Drenthe before and didn't even know that it had a village called Westerbork. We were surrounded by SS and police officers in the train who didn't let us out of their sight. I was wondering where they had sent Mrs. Nijsens. I never truly got to know her, apart from that one night when she told me about her husband. That was the most intimate our conversations had ever gotten. She was a tough woman, but nevertheless, she had a heart of gold. Keeping us inside her house, feeding us, and even taking care of her husband's bastard daughter. It gave me a feeling of guilt, knowing that she had been caught and that it might have been my fault. I tried to shake off the feeling, but it was constantly there, like a heavy block of stone resting in my stomach. I still felt anxious about our arrest. The images were flashing through my mind, and my heart was still palpitating with fear. I took a deep breath in and tried to relax. We hadn't slept since our arrest. My eyelids became heavy, and I felt a sudden need to rest. It might have been the long time spent on the train that made me realise how tired I was. Nico held my waist, and I put my head on his shoulder. Not a single word had been said throughout the whole train ride.

"You'll sleep when you arrive." One of the SS officers who spoke Dutch woke me up. He seemed to find pleasure in my unmet desire to rest, as if he was thinking that I had it coming. At that point, all my other thoughts had vanished. All I wanted to do was fulfil one of my basic needs. Even that, they were trying to take away from me. The urgent necessity to sleep.

AUTUMN, 1943—PART II

"GOOD MORNING, BEPPY!"

The bubbly fourteen-year-old Annie Bloem fed her new little sister and took her out for a walk through the parks of North Amsterdam. The family called their new sibling Beppy, for fear of being found out. During the walk, she described the landscape and all of their surroundings. Beppy kept pointing at everything and asking, "What's that?"

"The autumn leaves are floating through the air, surrounded by their deciduous trees. It is strange how, even though our lives and social circumstances change, the seasons will always remain the same," Annie explained. Little Beppy, who didn't understand that statement, just smiled and clapped her hands.

In the park, there was a group of scouts. "What's that?" Beppy asked again, pointing at the young boys and girls who were wearing pale-blue blouses, epaulettes, black shorts, or skirts and garrison caps, with ties for the boys.

"The National Youth Storm," Annie explained. The girl was incredibly clever and mature for her young age. She had a kind and nurturing character. Therefore, Annie had been given the responsibility of taking care of the twenty-month-old toddler who had been living with them for the past five months. Meanwhile, her family was trying to scrape together enough food and resources to get through the winter .

She was guiding Beppy's pram past the crowd, until they arrived at a bench. Annie took Beppy out of the pram and put her down to stand on both her feet. Annie sat on the bench and took a cheese sandwich out of her bag.

A few girls from the National Youth Storm came closer. They were charmed by the little Beppy who was trying to pull herself up.

"What's her name?" said a young girl with pigtails and a fringe.

Annie looked at Beppy. "Do you want to tell them?"

The girl crouched down and looked in her eyes. "Don't be shy."

Annie laughed. "Oh, trust me, Beppy is not shy." She held up one finger.

"The girl didn't ask for your age. She asked for your name." Annie repeated, "Your name!"

"Beppy!" she giggled triumphantly.

"Beppy is brown," another girl remarked.

"But she'll be whiter when she grows up!" the girl with the pigtails responded.

They enjoyed speaking to Beppy and getting a few responses out of her. Someone wanted to pick her up, but Annie refused. Then the girls were being called by their Scouts leader and felt disappointed about having to leave the little Beppy behind. When they were out of sight, Annie put her on her lap and looked her in the eyes.

"You are beautiful. Don't let anyone tell you otherwise."

We arrived in Westerbork and got off the train. The journey had been fairly quiet and our walk through the countryside was just the same. There were only sounds of wind, footsteps treading the soil, and an owl. We were walking in a line, surrounded by officers with torches. I had no idea what time it was or where exactly we were; for all I knew, we could've been in another country. It was so dark, we could barely see the signs, and the few that I could read were in German. Finally, we arrived somewhere where there were houses and buildings in sight, or so I thought. The officers had guided us to some sort of closed off village in the countryside. And the closer we got, the more I could see that it looked like an army camp rather than a village. I was so tired, to the point where I felt numb. I kept imagining myself sneaking out of the crowd and hiding in the bushes. It felt like a possible risk I could take, but Nico was walking in front of me, and I couldn't risk leaving him behind, let alone getting caught. The intrusive thoughts about what would happen if I were to get caught frightened me, and so I continued walking along.

We arrived in the "village" and had to wait outside a house-sized barrack. They sent people in, one by one. It was cold, and I didn't have enough layers on to keep me warm. Being tired and cold made me bad-tempered. I wanted to get angry at one of the soldiers and tell them to at least allow us to wait inside. I wanted to yell at them, tell them that I had always been a decent human being. That I had a daughter who was now growing up without her parents by her side. That it was all unfair. Nico turned to me and could sense my irritation. He came back over to my side and rubbed my back, gesturing that everything would be alright.

It was my turn to enter the barrack. There was a little office inside that reminded me of the one at the police station where I had been beaten. Entering a room with the same atmosphere immediately brought back the images of the officer hitting his fist into my stomach

and the female officer punching me. My lips still felt swollen, and I
all too well remembered the feeling of breathlessness and the nasty
taste in my mouth.

There was a woman behind the desk, but she seemed rather
friendly and harmless. Then again, you could never know for sure, so
I kept my guard up. Her manner of speech was strict, but there was
no physical harm involved. Just punching words and accusations,
which hurt just as much. She asked many questions—*Who are you?
Where are you from? Do you have any money or jewellery on you?
Were you in hiding?*

I stayed well-mannered and answered all of the questions she
asked me. She wrote down the answers and shook her head in
disapproval when I admitted to having been in hiding. I could've
lied, but I wasn't sure what Nico had told them, and I had this funny
feeling that they already knew this information but wanted to get
some more details out of me. She put a stamp on the document and
led me outside the office. I was given a pale overall and clogs, which
I had to put on. They negligently cut my hair very short. I couldn't
see myself, as there weren't any mirrors around, which was probably
for the best. Big chunks and strands of hair fell beside me. I would
have rather not seen how messy my hair looked in that moment. My
hair was cut shortly, to show everyone that I was a prisoner, a mark
of retribution and humiliation. After all, being a Jew in hiding was a
violation of the law, and this was my penalty. Together with the other
"inmates," including Feline, whose hair had also been cut short, we
were put inside the penal barrack 67.

The barrack was packed, and there were barely any beds left. I
wanted to sleep next to Feline but couldn't find a place where the
two of us would fit, so I had to cram myself in between two other
women who stank of unwashed sweat and soot. My back still hurt
from sleeping in Mrs. Nijsens' basement for all those months, and
this bed didn't help. I was softly sobbing. One woman next to me got
annoyed and kept telling me to be quiet. But I couldn't stop crying. I

wanted Nico to hold me and tell me it was going to be alright. I tried to change my thoughts and think about happy things. Tomorrow would be Saturday, the Sabbath, the Jewish day of rest. It took over my thoughts, and my crying slowly stopped as I remembered the smell of fresh challah bread, chicken soup, roast meat, and baked potatoes. The image of our family, sitting at the dinner table, chatting about mundane things, Nico getting annoyed at the lack of intellectual conversations and Ab provoking him in response, my mother, still alive, lighting the candles and singing a prayer, Father holding up a glass of sweet wine and toasting to us, the newlyweds.

Father . . . maybe he was here in Westerbork! Perhaps he could get me out of the penal barrack. But how could I find him?

And mother . . . we always said it was too soon for her to leave us, but looking back, I realised that her soul escaped just in time, to a good place, avoiding this bad dream.

And lastly, I thought of Betty, who guided me into a sweet slumber.

I gulped down the Saturday morning breakfast of Ovaltine and porridge before we had to go to work. Our barrack looked out on a barbed wire fence and a river. I imagined what it looked like on the other side, where people were walking freely in the open air.

The work was foul. We spent hours disassembling batteries and accumulators. Feline had been silent all morning, and she barely touched her breakfast. I tried to make conversation to lighten up the mood, but her expression had completely changed. A few days ago, at the Schouwburg, she had still been talkative, but now it seemed as though the life had been sucked out of her—as if she suddenly had the realisation that it would be a very long time until she'd see Boaz again, something which was completely out of her control.

During the work, I distanced myself from her. It seemed as though she didn't want company and would rather be lost in her own thoughts. Still, I needed some distraction. The work was disgusting and probably very unsafe. Most of us looked very ugly with our new haircuts and smelled bad due to the lack of soap. Nevertheless, the women managed to liven things up, engage in small talk, and have a laugh.

"I've always wanted to shave my hair off," said one of the girls, who was wearing a headscarf. She looked a little more like me, with similar Iberian features. "I have small breasts, so with my shaven head, I practically look like a man!" she continued enthusiastically.

"What's the first thing you would do as a man?" another woman asked.

"I'd just open a bank account," I replied. They all laughed.

"Or take out an insurance!" the girl said. She put her hand out. "Maria." It was covered in oil and grime.

"Hanna."

"That's my mother's name. I haven't seen her in a while."

"Where is she?"

"Somewhere in Westerbork."

"And you're not with her?"

"No, I did something stupid, and then I ended up here."

Maria seemed light-hearted and happy to answer my questions. I was curious as to what the camp was actually like, outside of the penal barracks.

"If I didn't know any better, I would assume that it almost feels like a small town," she explained about the facilities. There was a school, a hospital, a carpenter's shop, and even a small theatre. There was apparently a cameraman who was filming everything.

"Mother said that he's here to record the illusion of our 'peaceful' existence in Westerbork."

I wondered how it would have been had Nico and I not gone into hiding and just obeyed the orders. It crossed my mind for a few minutes, but then I realised how ridiculous I felt even considering the thought. Nothing about this whole situation had anything to do with justice. It wasn't about obeying the rules and getting a better deal. I felt a knot in my stomach thinking about how my father left without a trace.

"Is there a mental hospital around?" The chances were small, but I had to ask.

"Not that I'm aware of. Why?"

"My father might be here somewhere. Though he needs psychiatric attention."

"When did he arrive?" Maria looked doubtful.

"He was sent away in January."

Her face changed, as if she was trying to express that I should stop asking questions.

"If you don't say it, I will," another woman said to Maria.

"People leave this place. Every Tuesday, they shove as many people as they can into wagons."

I wanted to ask where to, but I was afraid of what the answer would be. "The free people on the other side are prisoners, too, just like us. They just don't realise it," Maria explained. I wanted her to know that I wasn't afraid and that I wanted to know the facts, no matter how hard they could be.

"An artificial city," I remarked.

"There are rumours that the trains are going to Poland, to a place far worse than the penal barrack in Westerbork."

"And my father?"

"I'm so sorry," she said. "I don't want to draw any conclusions, but giving false hope isn't any better."

The girls all went quiet, as if they all knew a person who had been sent away in the wagons.

"On Tuesday, they'll read a list with names. And we'll be at the top."

After the long work hours, we were finally back in our barrack. I kept thinking about father. If everything they had told me was true, then father probably wouldn't have survived the train ride. He was physically very weak, and I could not imagine him standing up in a train, packed with other people, for hours or even days. I tried to shake off my morbid assumptions.

It was just minutes before dinnertime and all the girls were already waiting outside the kitchen, but I was laying on a bed, taking pleasure in its spaciousness. It had only been one night, and I already craved my own sleeping space.

At dinner, Maria sat next to me. During one of our chats earlier, I found out that she was a Sinti. It baffled me that they were being maltreated, just like us. If we had met in our previous lives, then I'm not sure whether Maria and I would have been friends, or even noticed one another. But here, we both had one thing in common—being persecuted for who we were. I loved speaking to Maria; she had a childlike happiness to her but still appeared down-to-earth. A perfect balance of energy.

"You got a letter, Hanna," she said.

"What?"

It seemed highly unlikely for someone to know where I was, and for a second, I thought she was fooling me. And yet, it was true. Maria handed me an envelope which had my name on it and the address of the camp.

"How did you get this?" I was amazed and slightly shaken.

"Read it, and when you're ready, you can write a letter back."

"Can I do that?"

She gave me some writing material as well as an envelope.

"Don't keep it on you. Leave it somewhere hidden and give it back to me whenever you want. Normally, there is a postal service in the camp, but they are a bit less tolerant with people who are in the penal barrack for hiding."

"But how did you—"

"My mother believed that the Germans were reading everyone's letters before sending them. She is a very doubtful woman. But luckily, she found a nice guard who made sure our letters would arrive safely. He comes around to talk to me every once in a while. I think he's in love with me."

"Who is he? Are you sure you can trust him?"

"For safety reasons, it's best if you don't know his name. It's a chance you'll have to take."

I became hopeful and excited about the thought of who could have written to me. Was it Bonneka? Or maybe even Ab? My little brother and I hadn't communicated in a long time, and there was so much he needed to know. I didn't want to sugar-coat our situation to him. I took the materials and thanked Maria. I didn't know if I was ready to read it; my hands were shaking.

"I don't want to assume things, but try and write before Tuesday."

───────────

Nico looked about five years younger with his bald head. He felt self-conscious, like he wasn't being taken seriously. I still found him good-looking, but that didn't seem to matter to him. Our situation in Westerbork was very tough on him.

"They are treating us like sheep, shaving us of our comforts and pride, and forcing us to give our milk."

I told him about the writing materials which Maria had given me. We had been in Westerbork for only a day but realised that, if we didn't take action, we would be the next to go on the train. I thought long and hard about who to speak to and how to get ourselves out of this situation; after all, it was too dangerous to make mistakes.

I looked at Nico and wanted to kiss him so badly, feel his soft touch. But he seemed more preoccupied with his feeling of worthlessness. The same thing had happened to Feline, whereby her joy had deteriorated into a quick and sudden depression. But I couldn't let the same happen to Nico.

"My brother wrote to us."

He had a look of confusion but also somewhat lifted the corners of his mouth.

"What did he write?"

"Very brief and to the point, but could be useful to us."

I handed him the letter.

"Sounds like Ab."

> Sept 16, 1943
> Hansje and Nico,
> I found out from Mr. and Mrs. L that they caught you. I want you to know that B is safe, and so am I. You need to do all that you can in order to stay in Westerbork so that someone can get you out of there. Use your Sperre. I heard they need people like you to work. Show them your skills; it might help. Be brave, and don't let them get to you.
> All the best,
> Ab

"He wrote us three days ago! How has he found out?" Nico recognised Ab's handwriting but almost couldn't imagine the letter being real.

"The resistance is on our side" was all I could say.

Nico smiled, and for the first time since our arrest, he seemed hopeful again.

"On Tuesday, there will be another transport. We must do something before then," I insisted.

We only had two days to turn things around, which meant we had to act fast. I tried to assess whether I could give Nico a little kiss. We were both dirty, and I wasn't sure how he would react. I looked him in the eyes.

"We'll be okay," I told him, convincing myself as well.

He came closer and touched my lips with his.

"A good luck kiss, just in case," he whispered. We both smiled but had to part when we heard the footsteps of an officer approaching.

I ran around the building trying to find Maria. She was cleaning the floor of our sleeping barrack with a few other women. I grabbed her arm and asked if she could follow me into a corner of the room.

"What is it?"

"That officer," I spoke quietly. "I need to ask him for a favour."

"You can't do that."

"Please just tell me who he is, and I'll take care of it myself."

"That man is the one who is making sure my mother and I aren't put on transport. I don't want to risk it," she explained regretfully.

She had her priorities, and I understood that, but I had mine too.

"Maria, I have a daughter," I told her, something I had wanted to avoid mentioning. Her surprise showed me there was a small chance she would change her mind, but I would have to insist.

"You want to protect your mother, which I understand. But can you imagine how it must be for my daughter? Growing up, not knowing where her mother is."

Maria didn't respond. Had I pushed it too far? My sense of urgency might have made me lose my perception. After a couple minutes of contemplation, she came closer to my ear and whispered a name. I had a slight feeling of triumph. Nonetheless, I still had to hurry. I kissed her cheek to thank her and went outside the barrack. I knew which officer she had been talking about. He had been around the penal barrack, probably to see Maria. I wondered how I would speak to him. I couldn't just approach him; that could get me beaten up. I only had one shot, and I had to do it right.

He wasn't a handsome man, and I could understand why a pretty girl like Maria would charm him. Officer Schubber was muscular with a bit of a beer belly, yet his eyes were lidded and small. His nose was wider than the space between his eyes and his thin lips covered two front teeth which had a gap between them. My physical appearance wouldn't be of interest to him either, so I had to pull something off with my intellectual charm. I imagined all the different scenarios and things that could go wrong. Then I realised that using my smarts might not have been the best idea; maybe I had to play the helpless girl instead. But that didn't seem like a good idea either. Being a tall woman did not make me look particularly weak. Perhaps I had to focus more on his ego rather than my own and make him feel smart.

The moment I came closer and opened my mouth, he immediately put his defence up. He tried to stand tall and look down on me, even though we were the same height. I crouched down to make myself look smaller and more intimidated.

"Sir, is there any," I started, and he silenced me. This wasn't going to be a walk in the park.

"Go back to your hole, inmate!" he shouted, even though I was standing right in front of him. He probably wanted to prove his authority to the other officers and prisoners, who weren't even around.

I turned around to walk back but didn't want to admit defeat just yet.

"I have a solution to your problem," I said quietly, turning my head.

"Speak up, inmate!" he shouted again.

I fully turned around and spoke a little bit louder. "I have a solution to your problem." I was bluffing, of course. I wasn't sure whether he had an actual problem or not, but I had to test the waters.

This time, he was the one approaching me, and he spoke a little less loudly.

"What's your name?"

"Hanna, sir."

"And who are you?" He spoke patronisingly.

"Maria's friend."

This time, he observed me, as though he wasn't sure whether I was a Sinti or a Jew.

"What do you want?" He tried to sound normal, but I knew he was trying to hide the conversation from other officers.

"A chance to prove myself."

"Is there any point to your dull chatter?" He became a little bit more aggressive, and I had to come up with something good to say before I would lose him.

"I overheard the officers. You need more qualified administrators," I lied.

"You have no business listening to them!"

"I have a diploma in advanced typing and am an experienced accountant."

Again, he observed me, trying to figure out how I could be useful to him. He looked at the badge around my arm with the letter *S* on it. It stood for *Straf*, meaning punishment.

"That thing won't get you far, woman." He jerked his head down to my badge. "Do you think of yourself as superior to those qualified ones who haven't committed any crimes?"

That question didn't make any sense, and it showed his questionable level of intelligence, which frustrated me.

"Get out of my sight."

This time, I obeyed. He hadn't been as kind as I expected him to be.

Perhaps he really was in love with Maria.

When I returned to the barrack, she soon saw by the look on my face that I hadn't achieved anything.

"Can you talk to him?" I asked. She shook her head. I would have to find another way.

A thought came into my head. In the penal barrack, there were what we called the ODs, the *ordungdienst*, or order service. These were Jews who did the police's dirty work, by surveilling the penal barracks, where most officers didn't want to operate. The ODs were feared and hated, as they menaced their own blood just to avoid deportation.

I thought that if the German officers wouldn't listen to what I had to say, then perhaps they would. After all, they were just looking after themselves. If I found a way to make them believe that I could be of help, then I might avoid deportation myself.

———————

Sunday dinner was a watery soup with real potatoes, which felt like a big treat. I almost couldn't believe it. Even though I was thoroughly enjoying my meal, there was only one thing on my mind.

I was sitting opposite Feline, who just stared at her plate without touching her food.

"You should at least have one spoonful," I tried to tell her. She had barely eaten anything since we arrived.

"If I'm ill, they can't put me on the train," she uttered.

"If you're stick thin, you'll die before even getting on that train!" I pushed her plate towards her. She dropped her fork and looked annoyed. I suddenly had an idea, a selfish one, but worth a shot.

I stood up and looked at one of the ODs. He looked back, unsure what to think. I smiled, trying to see if he would accept flirtation, but instead, he just seemed disturbed. The paradox felt unreal to me, having to seduce a guard in order to survive, even though they were disgusted by our race. At least the ODs were just like us, and yet, they seemed to have adopted the Gestapo's mindset. When I looked back at him, I could see that he had noticed Feline, who was still frowning. That would be even more difficult, I thought, to try and convince Feline to help me.

"Why do you keep looking at him?" she lashed out.

"Can I trust you?" I knew the answer already but wanted to hear her say it first.

"What difference does it make?"

"Alright," I admitted. "I'm trying to prolong my stay at Westerbork."

"By becoming one of them? Good luck with that." She pointed at my *S* badge.

"I just need to speak to one of the—"

"I'm not interested," Feline interrupted distastefully. The way she spoke angered me. I hadn't done anything wrong and wasn't any happier about the situation than she. I had known Feline as a fun and bubbly character, but now she was just lifeless, patronising, and rude. I looked her in the eyes and stood up without saying another word. She didn't seem to mind and just crossed her arms. I took a deep breath and approach the OD.

"My friend told me you needed administrators," I lied again.

"I don't know what you're talking about."

"She overheard one of the guards."

"That friend?" he pointed at Feline. "Why? Is she an administrator?"

"No, but I am."

The man looked me up and down.

"And what do you want me to do?"

"Speak to Gemmeker."

I had heard guards say that name and, even though I didn't know who he was, I assumed that he was one of the big decision makers.

The OD laughed. "I can't just speak to Gemmeker."

"Fine, his advisors then," I tried.

"Sit back down."

It had taken me a lot of courage to speak to the OD, and I didn't want to return to Feline. But he looked away, as if I were a child that needed to be ignored in order to learn her lesson. I felt patronised yet again and left the kitchen. I tried not to cry but could not help myself. Was I really going to let them send me somewhere far away? All the way to Poland, just to let them continue treating me like a prisoner. I wiped away my tears and tapped my cheeks. There's only defeat in those who give up. The outside door was being opened, and I quickly hid behind a wall. Maria was entering the building, shortly followed by officer Schubber. She went into the kitchen, and he stayed in the hallway. I couldn't move and tried to hold my breath.

What had they been doing outside? I couldn't imagine her being that kind of person, but then again, who was I to judge? If I would have looked like her, or like Feline, would I have considered doing the same thing? After all, we were all trying to survive somehow. I would have to pretend I didn't see them entering the barrack, and maybe this was my chance to speak to him. At least now I knew for sure that he would be a little bit calmer. This was something I noticed with Nico, too. He was a quiet man, but very often had this inner tension that strangers could probably not sense. But I always felt it in him. And whenever we were intimate, it was as if his whole being was trying to get rid of this tension, only to experience a feeling of tranquillity afterwards. I never experienced this as intensely as him, so I assumed this must have been a phenomenon for men.

I pretended to walk towards the kitchen and acted surprised when I crossed officer Schubber.

"Your colleague asked for my details. Could I give them to you?" I tried to sound as calm and professional as I could. He shook his head, unbothered.

"Where do I go to work tomorrow?"

"The battery factory."

"Where's the barrack for the accountants?"

He seemed a little more interested. "Which colleague?"

"I don't know his name."

"Come to me tomorrow. I'll bring you to the barrack."

My heart did a little jump. Could I really avoid deportation?

Monday morning. The birds were singing, and so was I. Nico hadn't heard my news yet, as I hadn't wanted to tell him until things were certain.

However, I hadn't seen Schubber yet.

Nico was waiting in line for breakfast. When he had his food, I sat down next to him. He seemed happy to see me but exhausted too. At first, his main focus was on the plate in front of him, but then he looked up, as if he had some bad news to tell me.

"Have you sent the letter to your brother yet?"

"No, I'm waiting to write some positive news."

"Don't give it to your friend." He avoided eye contact.

"Why?"

"There have been some rumours." He was still looking down.

I didn't understand what he was talking about and asked him to look me in the eyes.

"Maria's a spy for Schubber."

"What for? She's a prisoner herself!"

"You are allowed to receive and send letters, even as a prisoner."

"But they might read them," I claimed.

"Why would that be of interest to them?" he asked genuinely. I didn't understand why we were having this conversation. Was there something I missed?

"Think about it. They don't care what you write; they care who you write to," he said. I took a long minute to think about it. Without saying another word to Nico, I left the table and went to work. I had tried to find Schubber, but he was nowhere to be seen.

Maria greeted me when she saw me. I asked whether she knew where he was.

"No, but have you written the letter?"

"Not yet," I admitted.

"Your family must want to know if you're alright," she said. I shook my head, and she seemed disappointed.

"It's just an old teacher asking whether I'm alright." I wasn't sure what use it was to her finding out who I wanted to write to. I still hadn't seen Schubber all day. Were they playing games with me? Trying to give me false hope? I felt foolish.

During the lunch break, I decided to confront her. "Why are you helping me?" I asked sceptically.

"I like you."

"What's in it for you?"

Maria didn't respond.

I decided to be blunt. "Are you spying on me?"

"Why would I be spying on you?"

"You tell me." This time I wasn't going to be treated like a half-wit. From when we were kids, Ab always told me that I put too much trust in others. I thought it was one of my better qualities, the fact that I cared about people and tried to give them a chance. But he was right—it had come back to bite me many times.

"Schubber is trying to find families who are still in hiding. And you're helping him!"

"I was just trying to—"

"God, Nico was right!" I snapped.

I wanted to act tough, but inside, I felt betrayed. Even though I had known this girl for less than a week, we had become very close and had spoken about personal things. I wasn't sure why she would want to deceive me.

"I had no choice," she tried to keep her voice low so that the others wouldn't hear what she was about to say. It seemed quite desperate, but I told myself not to fall for it.

"He brings me letters and tells me to try and get a name and address from who might be sending them and whether they're hidden Jews or part of the resistance. I don't choose who. I just obey."

So it was true. She did want to rat out where my family was hidden or who I had been in contact with. They were never going to put me to work in the camp's administration. I was a prisoner, an irritant they wanted to get rid of. Mrs. Nijsens had said that I should sometimes let go of my dignity in order to protect myself, but now it felt as if I didn't even have control over that anymore. It wasn't a choice whether I could keep my dignity or not; they would make that decision for me. When you're stripped away of everything, what can you hold on to?

That evening, I took out the writing materials and went looking for Nico. I needed him.

When I found him, the first thing I did was give him a kiss. I couldn't care less whether they would separate us or not.

"A good luck kiss," I said. "We'll need it."

From my expression, he probably understood that it was too late. Tomorrow would be Tuesday, the day of transport.

"I've seen the wagons," he said. "They're inhumane."

"We might be spared." I tried, but he seemed unconvinced. And so, we wrote.

Sept 20, 1943

Dear Ab,

As a goodbye, I am writing you this last note. We've seen the cattle trucks that are waiting for us. Unfortunately, the tip you gave us didn't work out. I have talked to several others, but with no result. For God's sake! We are very strong. Only thing is, I can't think about B, because that drives me insane, though it's for the best. We thank you for everything you've done for us. Take care. We hope to be back soon. Let Mrs. L take good care of B. Greetings to our acquaintances.

Lots of kisses from Hansje.

Greetings and all the best from Nico.

AUTUMN, 1943—PART III

MARIA WEPT FOR HOURS when she discovered that her mother
had been sent on transport two weeks ago. Officer Schubber was
nowhere to be seen, and there was no one who could help her. In a
way, I felt for her. She had humiliated me and taken advantage of my
trust, and yet I could not help but empathise with her situation. Her
mother was the last person who was still close to her, and there isn't
a stronger bond than that of mother and daughter.

"I guess it's my karma for betraying you." I could sense her
genuine sorrow. And yet, I wondered whether I would have done
the same, if it had been to protect my family. We had only been
at Westerbork for three days, but it felt like we had been there for
months. Time had gone by so slowly, and it was as if I had known
everyone there for a lifetime.

Maria, who was still crying, helplessly crawled down on the
disgusting floor. She laid there for a while, not knowing what to do

or what to feel. Everything she had fought for, every person she had betrayed—it was all for nothing.

They came to our barrack to read out the list, which was leaving on this specific Tuesday, 21 September.

Nico and I were on the list. Feline too. Maria wasn't. She stood up from the floor and shouted, "I want to go!"

I turned around and gave her a quelling look. It silenced her for a couple of seconds, until she started sobbing again.

The officers told us to gather our things and get ready to go on transport. One of them pointed at Maria and said, "You want to come. Be my guest."

Everyone whose name got called started getting ready to go on the train. I crouched down and grabbed Maria's arm.

"Stop acting like a fool!"

"That makes two of us." She was trying to make me angry, and I could see the pain in her eyes.

"She's been gone for two weeks. You might not even find her when you arrive."

"It's all my fault. I deserve to be on that train." She was squandering her chance of survival through self-pity.

I rested my hands on her shoulders, trying to grab her gaze. Maria could sense my eyes boring into hers, which eventually made her look up with uncertainty.

"You are brave. You are strong. You will not get on that train. You will survive and find your mother when this is over."

"Why are you helping me?" she sobbed.

"Because I have a daughter."

I kissed her forehead, stood up, and turned around to leave the barrack. There weren't many material things I had on me. No suitcase, no bag, no extra clothes, no jewellery, no money. Only the memories I carried with me.

Maria whispered, "Thank you," but I didn't look back.

The penal barracks hadn't smelled as bad as the wagon we were in during our train ride to the East. Fifty people pushed together like sardines in a tin. There was a young girl holding her child. She sang songs to the little baby, crying in her arms. Those who were standing close to her seemed annoyed by the baby, but I felt pain for the mother. It was dark in the wagon and, except for the mother humming to her child, the space was filled with a morbid silence. Nico was standing next to me, softly caressing my arm. He was touching my fingers and worked his way up to my elbow, trying to give me some feeling of comfort. It was his way of telling me that he would be there to protect me, no matter what.

The baby was still crying.

"Boy or girl?" I asked kindly.

"Girl."

"What's her name?"

"Shani."

She stopped crying.

My stomach was growling, but our wagon had made an unspoken agreement that we would leave the small amount of food that we had to those who needed it the most. We had no idea how much time we would be trapped in this small wagon, and how much longer we had to endure standing in the train.

I took Nico's hand, and we interlaced our fingers. At least I had him by my side, the man I loved. He had lost his glasses, his hair was shaven off, and he had a couple of bruises here and there. The train was dark, but I could still have him by my side. His handsome, charming self, a man who had been giving me unconditional acceptance and irreplaceable trust for so many years. There was a horrible smell and grotesque atmosphere, and yet, I could not help but think about the moments I fell in love with Nico. I still found it difficult to believe that I could call this man my husband. He was looking away, deep in thought, and got surprised when I kissed his cheeks. He turned around and kissed my lips. The baby started crying again. That kiss was an escape from our surroundings, a confirmation that we still loved each other, and that no matter what would happen, we'd be there for one another.

Seconds, minutes, hours passed by. We weren't sure whether there was light or darkness outside, early morning, late afternoon, or the middle of the night. I tried to hold my bladder, but it became more and more difficult as time passed by. Only one guy had used the little bucket in the corner of the wagon. No one had looked at him or even glanced for a second; we didn't want to be judgemental. Nonetheless, the old man had a look of shame afterwards. He must have been a decent middle-class man, as his speech was eloquent, and his manners refined. The sort of man my father would have done business with in the old days, when he still had his company and fortune. But hearing this man pee into a bucket immediately changed that image. It was strange how such a small gesture could unconsciously change your opinion of a person. Seconds before the look of shame, there was also a slight smirk of satisfaction. He had broken the ice for those needing to go as well, because afterwards, a few other people peed. For women, it was even harder, having to squat down. It might have been an immature thing of me, but I wanted to wait until Nico had peed. The thought of peeing in a train full of strangers wasn't what would embarrass me. It was idea that Nico would be there to witness the act that would feel denigrating. Therefore, I tried to hold it in for as long as I could.

Does this guy have an iron bladder? I thought, observing Nico, wondering whether he would have to go soon. This time, I couldn't hold it any longer. Without looking him in the eyes, I wrung myself between the crowd of people towards the bucket. They all looked annoyed, knowing another person would have to pee. I came closer to the bucket and saw that it was three quarters full. I didn't want to be the person who would make it overflow. I crouched down to a squat and tried really hard not to make a sound, which was very difficult. I just about emptied my bladder and didn't overflow the bucket. Surprisingly, there was no feeling of shame, just relief and sadness. Never in a million years would I have imagined that it would come to this, that I would stay hours on a train full of silent people, worrying about peeing in a bucket.

I got closer to Nico again. We locked eyes, and in his smile, I saw uncertainty—a dubious expression which I had seen before.

"Hold that stare. I'm taking a picture!"

Selma sat across from us at a terras in Noordwijk. A warm and sunny afternoon in the salty air. It was one of my favourite places to be during the early summer. Selma's camera made a clicking noise, and she told us we could drop the pose now.

"I'm calling it 'Noordwijk in conversation'," she smiled.

Nico and I were still looking at one another. We had been discussing the Netherlands' politics. There had been a cabinet crisis because of the increase in international tensions, and I thought that due to their internal problems, it wouldn't take long before the minister's different opinions would drive the cabinet apart. It was all the prelude to a bigger conflict to come.

Nico listened attentively, occasionally arguing, saying that there was a possibility of combining their ideas: new budget cuts did not exclude ideas for employment opportunities. "Their egos are too wide for a cooperation. One of them will step out," I said. Nico always listened to me and spoke in a way that made me feel intelligent. He was always interested and never undermined my arguments. We had been in a serious relationship for a while now. My friends seemed slightly jealous and couldn't stop talking about his charms. He was a quiet man, but still waters run deep.

I was wearing a white button-through summer dress, with a flirty flower pattern and a matching hairband, an outfit which I knew he loved. Nico never told me, but his eyes explained it all, and every time I wore that dress, he couldn't take them off me.

"We're going to put our feet in the water. Do you want to join?" Selma asked.

"Maybe later," Nico replied.

They nodded and went off to the shore.

"Shall I get some more iced tea?" I asked.

"Do you want to marry me?" He took me by surprise.

It would be a terrible time to do so—we were both working low wage jobs, our families were financially unstable, the country's government was on its head, and there was a war going on in Europe.

Nico knew I was considering all the worst outcomes and looked at me with uncertainty. He put his hand on my lap. "I know how much you want to start a family." He was right about that.

My worries did not take away the fact that all I wanted was to be with Nico. "Of course, I want to marry you!"

He sighed in relief and kissed me. "A kiss for our good fortune," he said.

"Rather a kiss for our luck. You'll have to convince my father first." I laughed.

"He'll come around. Your mother will convince him." Nico kissed my cheek. "A good luck kiss."

I couldn't wait to tell the others.

That was four years ago, but still so fresh in my memory—the way he had stared in despair after asking the question. Later, he even told me that he thought I would say no. Apparently, I had seemed more hesitant than excited. Still to this day, I could not have imagined myself doubting whether I wanted to marry Nico, even with everything going on.

That memory, that feeling, it took me back to Noordwijk for a split second. Until Shani started crying again. The smell of piss and sweat arose, and I was surrounded by miserable frowns.

Arbeit macht Frei—work makes you free—said the sign. I wondered what they meant by that. We had gotten off the train and walked through the mass of people, holding hands. There were families, young couples, elderly . . . *How many people could they shove into a train, and where are they all coming from?* I thought. The fact that I had Nico next to me made feel a little bit more like an actual human being, like a woman. Not another sheep in the flock. Further away, we could see that the men and women were being separated. "Just like in Westerbork."

"It's alright. We'll hopefully see each other for supper." I forced a smile. He grabbed me by the shoulders and went in for a tight hug. We whispered that no matter what happens, we love each other dearly. "Think of Betty," he said. "And whatever you do, don't waste a tear on those bastards."

I thanked Nico for his advice. "And you be strong," I told him. "Use your best muscle." I pointed at his forehead.

"*Weitergehen!*" someone shouted at us.

We let go of one another and had to separate, Nico in the men's queue, and me in the women's. I had wanted to give him a last good luck kiss but was scared of someone shouting at us again. *I'll give him one later*, I thought, *something to look forward to.*

In the queue, I saw Feline again. She had been put on another wagon, and the last time I had seen her was at Westerbork. There were a couple of people in between us. "Psst, Feline," I whispered. The people in front turned around, and one of the women put her hand on Feline's shoulder. She turned to face me. I gestured for her to come next to me, and she did.

"We're in this together."

She didn't respond, but I could see her eyes watering. How she had acted in Westerbork didn't matter at this point. What mattered was that we would continue taking care of each other. It was nice to be around a familiar face, and she probably felt the same.

There was a man in a white lab coat sitting down. The man had sleek black hair and was clean-shaven. He told every person passing whether they had to go to the right or to the left. I noticed a pattern to his choosing. Teenagers and young women to the right, mothers, small children, and elderly to the left. A couple of young women were sent to the left too. They were skinny and seemed almost too weak to stand. In Westerbork, there had been two types of prisoners—those who were allowed to wander freely and those who had to stay in the penal barracks. It seemed like no one knew I had been a prisoner there, as if I had a clean slate.

I had a funny feeling about this situation and thought about the sign which we had seen at the entrance. *Work makes you free.* It could be a metaphor. The people who went to the left were those that didn't seem fit enough to work. I looked at Feline, who had become even skinnier with protruding bones. I took off my jumper and told her to wear it. She didn't understand why I wanted her to put it on. She was already wearing warm enough clothes, and besides, I was much taller than her, and my jumper would be way too big. And yet, she saw my concern, and without saying a word, she put it on. With the jumper, she looked slightly more full-bodied and muscular.

The mother from our wagon and her daughter Shani were in front of the man. He led them to the left, following the path of those unfit to work, I assumed. Again, I had a hunch that the left path was no good and felt a pain in my chest seeing all those kids holding their mother's hands and happily following them. From what I remembered others saying, we had been sent here to the East to work. Therefore, I wasn't sure whether the line of mothers, babies, children, and middle-aged women was one I wanted to be in.

It was our turn. Feline and I didn't look alike at all. She was small and fair-skinned, whereas I was darker and much taller. The man looked us up and down, fascinated by our physical differences.

"*Schwestern?*" he asked.

Feline spoke a little German and replied, "*Freundinnen.*"

I hadn't heard her speak with such a powerful voice and

confidence in a long time. She probably understood that, in order to survive, she had to appear resolute.

It worked, because the man pointed his thumb to the right—the working path.

We had to strip naked, and our hair got shaven off.

"Maria would've loved this," I joked, and Feline giggled. It briefly made me happy to finally see her respond again. Now that we only had each other to rely on, there was a genuine sudden shift in her mood. I wasn't sure what exactly affected her to be more engaged and less irritable. Nevertheless, I felt blessed to have her by my side.

"What actually happened with Maria?"

"She was too clever for her own good, and I too gullible for mine," I answered honestly.

Feline stared at my shaven head and commented on how I looked better without that horrible haircut they had given me in Westerbork. I didn't believe her but appreciated the gesture.

We waited for hours, naked in the cold. Feline's body was half the size she had been when I first met her. Her bones still accentuated her hips and other places where there had been curves before, but that was also the problem. There was more bone than flesh. My stomach rumbled again. I had forgotten how hungry I was.

After a very long wait, we finally received some pyjamas. They didn't look very clean, but they gave us some warmth in the cold autumn air. We had to wait outside again.

"Do you think this place will be like the penal barracks in Westerbork?" Feline wondered. I looked up at the black smoke covering the sky. A woman standing close to us laughed mockingly. She was Dutch and understood what we had been saying.

"Westerbork is purgatory, and after that, there are only two destinations."

WINTER, 1943

"YOU ADD THE WHITE CASTER sugar to your pot with a pinch of salt. Also make sure the flour is half plain, half self-rising, and don't throw all of it in at once! You just use one whisked egg and kneed in the cold, creamy butter. It usually helps to cut the butter in pieces before kneading. Press the dough in a greased tin and bake it until golden brown."

It was nighttime and our barrack had not received dinner that evening, as all our bowls had miraculously disappeared. We assumed that this was done by some of the guards, who were trying to mess with us. About a month ago, when I first arrived at the camp, I could hardly swallow the repulsive liquid which they called *soup*, but after having been there for almost three months, I could hardly endure its absence.

"Ladies, my recipe for blintzes is to die for!" Tony beamed. She was a German who spoke a little bit of Dutch. We had become friends.

Tony was a beautiful woman with an incredibly amusing personality. In the barrack, we called her Carole Lombard, as she almost looked identical to the actress. Except that Tony was much shorter. A tiny woman with a big character. During our chat about recipes, Feline remained quiet. She lay down on the wooden bunk planks which we had to call our beds. She had been ill for a couple of days; most people seemed to have difficulty coping with the cold. But Feline was particularly weak these days. She still pretended to be strong during the daytime when we had to work, but at night, she would collapse in our barrack. Her stomach had also shrunk a lot; she could barely keep in any food, unless she thoroughly chewed it first.

Whilst Tony was telling us about blintzes, everyone looked at her in awe, and I was sure their mouths were watering, just like mine. I had tried to involve Feline in the conversation, but soon realised there was no point. She just had to rest.

We heard footsteps from outside, and before we realised it, our barrack doors were slammed open. Tony was the only one who spoke German and usually translated for our barrack. They were doing the usual dreaded check-up, so we had to go outside in the freezing cold and stand in line.

"You shiver, you get shot," Tony translated. The female officer walked past, counting us, whilst directing her eyes from our heads to our feet. I glanced at Feline, who could barely keep herself up.

"Take off your clothes," the officer instructed. Feline did as she was told, and we all looked at her with disbelief. She was trying so hard to stand still.

"Now run in a circle!"

The officer seemed unimpressed by Feline, who kept stumbling over her own feet.

"Faster!"

Feline tried. She ran as fast as an underfed dog would run after food, if they had chains attached to their feet.

Some of the girls looked down, but the officer kept shouting at us to watch the spectacle. I wanted to say something, scream, and tell her to leave Feline alone. The words were there, on the roof of my mouth, but my tongue felt stuck. She had a gun, she could shoot me, or worse, she could shoot Feline.

So, I watched. Unable to do or say anything. Nevertheless, I was impressed by Feline's endurance.

"Stop!" she shouted. The officer must have felt slightly defeated as Feline was still standing. She could've shot Feline, right then and there, but must've thought it would be more humiliating if she had to stay alive.

Afterwards, Feline was lying next to me on the straw bedding. "I don't want to do it anymore," Feline said. "I can't." She was shivering.

"I wanted her to shoot me."

Hearing her say those words hurt me. I gently caressed Feline's cheeks, trying to comfort her.

"You are so strong—"

"I don't want to be strong. I want to go home."

I felt the same way. My nose started twitching, and I felt my stomach turn. I thought that I'd start crying, though my eyes could not produce a single tear. I strongly felt an urge to let it all out, but it was as if my body was stopping me from doing so.

"Boaz would want you to stay alive."

"Boaz wouldn't want to see me suffer."

I thought of Nico, wondering how he was holding up. We hadn't seen each other since our arrival. I missed his touch.

———

We found out about the gas chambers. I prayed that they hadn't sent Nico on the left line that day when we arrived. He was such a good person. I could imagine him helping an older man walk and accidentally sending himself to his death too. The thought frightened me, and I tried to shake it off.

Feline noticed my thoughts drifting. "What's on your mind?"

"Our freedom. The day we'll walk out of here and go back to Amsterdam."

"Will you teach me to make *boterkoek*?"

"The best one you've ever had."

Soon after, Feline fell asleep, and I could hear her breathing heavily next to me. It was a comforting feeling, knowing that she was asleep, unaware of her surroundings. A brief moment of peacefulness.

For me, that peacefulness came when I reflected on Betty's freedom. She was almost two years old and probably already learning how to say short sentences. I assumed she was calling the woman taking care of her, "mum." I hoped they played the piano. She liked that. I wished I was the one playing for her.

The next morning, I tried to wake up Feline, but she didn't move. She just lay there, still. Her skin was cold, and her body seemed heavy and flaccid. I pressed my fingers to the side of her neck. I had always been an easy crier, but again, my eyes felt numb and didn't produce a single tear. Tony gestured that I should quickly get up. I pointed at Feline's lifeless body. Tony covered her mouth and gasped in shock. We stared at one another, not knowing what to do. We had to leave her body behind in the bed and go outside.

Feline's brief moment of peacefulness had turned into an eternal blissful slumber.

I wasn't able to allow myself a single moment of grief, and I marched to work. Tony held my hand.

They led us to an old warehouse which had been turned into a storage facility. We were on Kanada-commando, one of the least awful jobs in the camp. Tony and I stayed close to one another, whilst organising and clearing up all the belongings of those who had just arrived at the camp. The guard who stood close to us was continuously eyeing Tony, who still looked like a Hollywood actress, even with her sloppy headscarf and muddy face. She kept her head down, and I knew she felt uncomfortable. It was true that I rarely saw ordinary women as beautiful as Tony. And this would be even less likely in a prison camp. The guard was called away by one of the officers to check on a prisoner who had stolen something. Tony seemed more at ease when the guard had finally left, even though she knew that it meant the supposed thief would be sent to the gas chambers or shot. That thief's condemnation was Tony's temporary moment of relief.

"What is Tony short for?" I tried to make conversation. "Tamara." She smiled. "What's Hansje short for?"

"Hanna."

"Such a beautiful name. Why would you want to change it?"

"From when I was little, people always called me that."

"Do you mind if I call you Hanna?" she asked, and I shook my head.

"Your Dutch is remarkable," I noticed.

"I lived in Amsterdam in 1935."

"To escape Germany?"

There weren't many other reasons for a woman to leave her home country during the war.

"I would never let my unborn daughter grow up in a country that despises her existence."

She noticed my stiffening posture.

"Do you have children?" she asked casually.

"A daughter." My voice was shaky.

"So, you must understand my reasoning." I nodded.

"But we had to leave Amsterdam when my husband got a job in Belgium," she stopped herself. "Forgive me. I tend to mix up Dutch and French."

It was true that her sentence structures and use of words were odd at times, but I was still very surprised by all the languages she spoke. Not only was Tony stunning and charming, but she was intelligent too.

"If I had stayed in Amsterdam, I might have seen you sometime."

"I'm sure we would have been friends." Tony had a pleasant laugh.

"Maybe I wouldn't be here now," she was more sincere. "But the past is the past."

I thought that if I'd tell her something personal, she might feel less afraid to open up.

"I had to give my one-year-old daughter to strangers."

She looked at me with slight admiration.

"One must not underestimate the power of being a mother." Another guard came closer, and we continued working. This one was eyeing Tony too. I could sense her discomfort and even wondered whether one of these men had done something to her.

We worked in silence until it was finally time for our short lunch break. Tony and I grabbed our bowls and stood in the cue for food. We had been waiting for a while, and I was tapping the floor with my foot, anxious that we would have to go back to work without having had any food.

"Have you heard anything from your husband?" I asked, trying to distract myself.

She looked around to make sure people weren't listening, even though no one could understand the language we were speaking.

"He escaped," she whispered.

"How?"

"Zigbert ran to the roof before they could catch him. It was too late for me—"

She stopped herself.

"Is your husband safe?" Tony asked.

I shook my head and she looked down.

Finally, it was our turn to receive food. We presented our bowls and received a single spoonful of potato peel soup and black bread with margarine. It was a male prisoner who was giving out the food. He sneakily poured Tony another spoonful and gave her an extra piece of bread.

There was a slight drizzle of rain, and we sat down on the muddy floor to eat our lunch. She split her second piece of bread and gave me the other half.

"Your admirers are keeping us well fed," I joked.

Tony laughed audibly. We quickly gulped down our food.

"Your daughter, is she still with those strangers?" she asked.

"I hope so. And your little girl, she must be with her father?"

"Frieda was with her nanny in the park the day the Gestapo came for us. When I was at the transit camp, I looked everywhere to see if they had been caught too."

She let out a deep sigh.

"But thank God, they were not there. I believe they're hidden somewhere."

"You were betrayed, weren't you?"

Those were the most common stories of those who tried to escape the transport. It had happened to me, and I was almost certain it happened to Tony too.

"By a neighbour and friend," she admitted painfully, "Jacques."

I could see her emotions toppling outside of her mind, as though she was unleashing her hatred upon this man. She spat on the floor, which shook me. It was a very unladylike thing to do, especially for such an elegant woman such as Tony. I was surprised, and it made me even more intrigued by her.

"Joeri," I said. "That's the man who ratted us out. There's something about that letter *J* that makes them want to betray."

Tony forced a smile. The officers ordered us all to go back to work. It was difficult, trying to understand the officers and guards. They only spoke in German, and though I had learned a little bit of the language in school, I often found myself too worried to pay attention to what they were saying.

"Can you teach me German?" I asked Tony. She accepted my request. During the rest of our shift, she only spoke to me in German, and whenever I said a word in another language, she pretended not to understand.

When we got back to the barrack late that night, Feline's body was gone. I whispered a little mourning prayer and thought about Boaz. That night, I had difficulty falling asleep. In my mind, I was going over what I would tell Boaz about Feline's death. Naturally, the first thing I'd tell him would be about how brave Feline was and how peaceful her death had been. Two things that weren't necessarily true but would help with his grieving.

No one knew it was my birthday, and I wanted to keep it that way. But, in my mind, I had made a wish. I knew I wanted something to change.

My wish eventually came through but not the way I thought it would. Something changed when a man in a white doctor's coat entered our barrack. I remembered him from the day when we had arrived at the camp. His uniform was still polished, and his hair gelled back neatly. He was accompanied by a group of assistants, who were all standing behind him.

There was a feeling of fright in the barrack—was he going to send some of us to the gas chambers? Everyone was thinking that. The man observed us thoroughly, with an air of superiority, unlike the one we had seen in the officers. He was calm and collected—I would even say *charming*. But his attitude was that of a person who knew exactly where he was standing and what he could do. I assumed he was a doctor, a man capable of choosing who to spare and who to let go of. He smiled at us, exposing the gap between his front teeth.

One of the men behind him paid a great deal of attention to me. His deep dark eyes seemed to examine my body assiduously. He said something to the doctor. All I could understand was that he was speaking about "the very tall one," which I assumed was me. Whilst he spoke, the man occasionally smiled, exposing his dimpled cheeks.

"Who here can dance or play an instrument?" the doctor asked respectfully. I had heard from other inmates that those who had any particular talents were usually kept alive for longer as they were a good source of entertainment for the Germans. And ever so often, they received extra food. I slowly put my hand up, hoping that I wasn't fooling myself. The man with the dimples seemed pleased by this and asked me to step forward.

"Piano," I murmured. No one else had stepped forward, and it made me feel ashamed. Was I really going to share my musical passion with these people, or was this a trap? The doctors, however, seemed impressed and left the barrack.

"This might have been the smartest thing you've done or the dumbest," Tony whispered.

A month passed and nothing else like that night happened. My German had gotten significantly better, and I was finally able to understand most of it and say basic sentences.

One very early morning when our barrack door was opened, the man with the dimples was back. Another woman next to him ordered us to stand in line and present ourselves to the doctor. He noticed me again and gestured that I should take a step forward. Then he pointed at two other girls from our barrack and told them the same thing. This way, he had picked out three people: Hilla, Tillie, and me. Hilla and Tillie were twin sisters and clearly looked like minors. They were Roma.

Tony and I glanced at one another. In a way, that moment reminded me of my time in high school, when we had to be separated into teams during our sport matches in P.E. class. This time, my friend and I hadn't been chosen to be on the same team.

We were told to follow the man. I glanced at Tony, who looked concerned. I wondered where they were taking me, and whether this was in favour of my safety or to my detriment.

Outside, there were a dozen other women who would join us. We left our wooden barrack and had to cram ourselves into a truck which drove for more than twenty minutes. It was so far away from our previous barrack, I couldn't imagine having to do this journey every day. I wanted to go back. We had created a routine for ourselves there. It was a terrible place of inhumanity, and yet, it felt more secure and oddly familiar. At least there I knew the rules and what I had to do to survive. I had already gotten used to the wake-up gong at four thirty in the morning and jumped out of bed to start cleaning the barracks. The naked walks to the bathhouse in the cold winter mornings became one of the camp's lesser evils, and I would force myself to look forward to the sludge they called coffee.

It was all a pretence, for I had long realised what they really wanted to do with us. There had been rumours going around, and everyone knew it. This so-called work camp was there to mask the fact that this place was utterly a killing centre. We weren't forced labourers—we were prisoners awaiting execution. I looked down at my arm, which had been tattooed with the number 63228. It had become my new identity. My name no longer mattered.

The truck arrived at a place where we were surrounded by solid brick masonry buildings. I wondered how long we were staying here and whether this was only a place to work or our permanent sleeping accommodation. A few of the assistants came to separate us into two groups. The doctors and assistants were discussing things internally. Though, thanks to Tony, my German was finally good enough, and I could understand everything they said. The assistants were asking a certain man, who they referred to as Dr. Mengele, whether he wanted to keep the group or send them to the gypsy camp.

The doctor was the man in the white coat, who I remembered from our arrival at the camp, as well as the day he and the other men entered our barrack. The man with the sleek haircut who had smiled at us, exposing the gap between his teeth. Behind him was a line of children, all twins, holding hands. The children, who looked surprisingly excited, were surrounded by a couple of prisoners, who I assumed were the doctor's assistants. He examined us all and remembered me.

"*Der pianist*," he pointed out happily. It was the first time in a while that I felt like a dignified human being. This doctor spoke like and seemed to be a decent man. Still, I was trying to keep my guard up, for I knew there was no such thing as decency here.

The guards took the other group of girls away, including Hilla and Tillie. After which the doctor left too, followed by his entourage of twins.

Some of the Jewish prisoner assistants took us inside one of the solid masonry type houses. On the first floor, we found our new sleeping area. The guards explained that we had to receive medical check-ups, and I was the first one lined up for it. I had to go to the ground floor and wait until I was allowed to enter the doctor's room.

In there, the man with the dimpled cheeks was sitting in front of me, asking basic questions.

"What's your name?"

"How old are you?"

"What kind of sports have you done in the past?"

"Do you have a history of medical problems? Perhaps in your family?"

"Do you have any siblings? Any twins?"

"Are you married?"

"How many sexual partners have you had?"

Then one question took me by surprise. "Have you ever given birth?" The doctor could see my struggle when trying to give an answer.

"Don't panic," he said. "I just want to understand which physical and hormonal stresses your body has gone through."

"Yes," I answered. "I have given birth." His eyes lit up.

"When?"

"Almost two years ago."

"What happened to it?"

The fact that he called my baby *it* sickened me, but it also forced me to carefully choose my words.

"She died." I felt a lump in my throat.

He told me he was sorry, and I didn't believe a word of his pretence. This man was out to get me. I had felt safe for a brief moment but could thankfully see more clearly now. *Don't fall for his traps*, I told myself. *It will be the death of you.*

After the questions, he asked me to strip down naked for a medical examination. His assistant measured and weighed my body. I felt ashamed but tried not to show it. The stronger I appeared, the less pleasure he would get out of degrading me, I hoped.

"Hanna," he said, "I forgot to introduce myself."

I was standing there naked and ashamed—the last thing I wanted to know was this man's name.

"Call me Dr. Schumann."

"Yes, doctor."

He didn't allow me to put my clothes back on; instead, he ordered me to lay down on the medical table in the middle of the room. I was placed in between two large devices, which pointed at my pelvis.

I panicked, and my breathing quickened. *Calm down*, I thought, *it's only temporary*. The man came closer and turned on the devices.

"Don't you worry. The X-ray machine is for a check-up. It will only take a couple of minutes."

The machine made a loud noise, and its beam felt like it was burning my skin. The doctor hadn't lied, the X-ray only took two minutes, after which he thanked me, gave me a few pills to swallow, and sent me back to the sleeping block.

On the way, I asked the assistant what he had just done.

"Don't worry about it," he told me. "For now, it means you get to live."

That evening, we received black bread, margarine, and sausages. Even though I couldn't wait to tuck into the food, my body started feeling strange. I felt a terrible stabbing pain in my uterus, almost three times more painful than a normal menstruation. Not now! I finally had some proper food in front of me. I was scared that if I would leave to the bathroom, my food would be gone by the time I returned. I shoved the food in my pocket and ran to the latrines. They were all being used, and I had to wait.

"My stool has been like this for weeks. They are poisoning our soup!" A woman complained to her friend who was on the latrine next to her.

When it was finally my turn, my lower stomach was hurting so bad, it felt as if the menstruation blood would come pouring out of me. But there was nothing. I shrieked in pain, not knowing what to do.

The woman who had been complaining swiftly turned to me and helped me get up. "Did they inject you?" she asked. I shook my head, unable to respond. My whole uterus felt like it was going to explode. The girl led me back to the bunk beds where she helped me lay down.

"Can someone get Gina?!"

I could barely move. Other girls were now standing over me.

"She's boiling," one of them shouted.

My eyelids became heavier and heavier, I couldn't keep them open, and slowly but surely, they dropped, only leaving me in the darkness of my own sockets. I still heard the girls around me panicking, but their voices gradually diminished until I could only hear my own heart beating in my ears.

I wasn't fully sleeping but transported to another place—that undistinguishable limbo between slumber and wakefulness. In the limbo, someone was standing over me, holding Betty. It was a young girl. She was cradling the little Betty, singing a lullaby to make her fall asleep.

"Sleep Beppy, sleep,
Outside, there is a sheep.
A sheep with little white feet,
Who drinks its milk so sweet.
Sleep Beppy, sleep,
Outside, there is a sheep . . ."

Betty was crying for her mother, and the girl had disappeared. She was sitting on the floor, by herself, continuously crying.

"I am here!" the young girl said sweetly. "Don't you worry."

I was trying to get closer, but I couldn't. I didn't want the people behind me to get to my child. The girl was taking good care of her. She turned around and saw me.

"Hansje, it's alright," she said. "Beppy is my little sister. I feed her, bathe her, walk her, and let her sleep in my bed."

I cried, "My baby . . ."

Nico put his hand on my shoulder and wiped my tears away.

"Don't waste a tear on those bastards."

Ab was looking at the young girl taking care of little Betty, only he was on the other side of the room, shaking his head disapprovingly.

"Hansje, you're too sensitive! You were the one who wanted this; now take responsibility for it."

Mother was standing next to Ab, smiling. "You created such a beautiful thing. Isn't she beautiful, Mozes?"

Father nodded and gave mother a kiss. "A treasure she is. Take good care of her, Annie."

The young girl nodded and looked at me.

"She's in good hands, patiently waiting to see you again soon." The girl, Annie, left the room, holding Betty in her hands whilst singing the lullaby.

"Sleep Beppy, sleep,
Outside, there is a sheep.
A sheep with little white feet,
Who drinks its milk so sweet.
Sleep Beppy, sleep,
Outside, there is a sheep . . ."

I opened my eyes, laying on one of the bunk beds. The room was empty, and I felt incredibly thirsty. There was a bowl with water next to me. I tried to sit up, but my whole body felt stiff. Something smelled terrible. I checked my pockets and found the piece of bread and sausage, which were mouldy. I felt too weak to throw them away, so I put them back in my pocket. After a few minutes, I finally managed to push myself up to sit. I took the bowl of water and slurped it. It satisfied me. My body ached, and my skin felt itchy. Where was everyone? How long had I been asleep?

I lied back down for what felt like an hour, trying to slowly move my body.

"She's awake!"

"Who are you?" I asked in German.

"Kay."

The woman sat down next to me and put her hand on my forehead.

"Good afternoon, warrior," she spoke in Dutch.

"The others told me about my Dutch competition," Kay said sarcastically. My vision was still a bit blurry, so I couldn't properly see what she looked like, though her voice was very gentle.

"How long have I been sleeping?" I whispered.

"A couple of days, but your fever is gone!"

She gave me a piece of bread and told me to chew slowly.

"What happened?"

"You're alive. That's all that matters," she caressed my forehead.

"Kay managed to convince the doctors to keep you," a woman explained proudly. I was still too weak to express my gratitude, so I just nodded with a sincere smile.

"Don't thank me yet," Kay warned. "Quid pro quo."

Later, I found out that Dr. Schumann wanted to see me when I had woken up. He wanted to do a few more tests on me. The girls promised they wouldn't tell that I was awake until I had fully recovered. I spent the next couple of hours trying to stand up and eat some more. The girls had all spared a little bit of their bread to give me. It wasn't much, but I felt grateful for it. Besides, I had difficulty swallowing, so it was probably best to only have small quantities for now.

Kay had been taking care of me for all this time, simply because we were both Dutch. When my vision came back, I could finally see her more clearly. Her face was long and tired, and she had big bags under her eyes. Still, something about her was enchanting. There was a comfort in her shimmery hazel eyes which were framed by her long batting eyelashes. Though her hair was wrapped in a scarf, I could still see a few light-brown strands escape the cover. Kay sat next to me for that entire afternoon, and we spoke about so many things. It was the first time since I last saw Tony that I could speak in Dutch to someone. It felt incredibly liberating to talk to Kay about our past and all the cultural things we had in common.

That same evening, I already had my energy back. It was miraculous how quickly I had recovered. Still, I didn't know what had caused this immense pain and fever. Was it the X-ray machines, or the food? I still had some menstruation pains, but I checked my trousers, and there was no blood. My body also itched. I rolled up my sleeves and was repulsed by the sores on both my arms. My chest itched too, and I checked to find that that part of my skin was also covered in pus-filled blisters.

A woman named Gina told me not to worry. She had apparently been applying an ointment to my rashes and said that they would heal in a few weeks.

"Just make sure to cover them up, and don't ever mention my name to the doctors!"

I gave her my word and said I would be careful.

"Dr. Schumann wants to see you tomorrow."

My hands started sweating, and I felt dizzy at the thought of seeing the doctor tomorrow. A feeling in my stomach was telling me the worst was yet to come.

WINTER, EARLY 1944

ON THE DAY of Betty's second birthday, I softly whispered a birthday song. Her smile was constantly on my mind. That morning, I had been ordered to Dr. Mengele's music room. He wanted me to play the melodies from Schubert's repertoire. He ordered me to play the first song. My sleeves were covered, as I didn't want the doctor to notice my rashes. They had been curing very slowly, and Gina, the nurse, still applied an ointment almost every day.

My fingers were rapidly pressing the keys, producing the classical sound that Dr. Mengele loved so much. He took out his violin and joined. This was the second time I had been asked to play for him. The girls warned me that I should not dare to anger the doctor, as he apparently carried an infamous temper. He didn't appear to be an angry person—simply a lover of music, who wanted to make the most out of having talented slaves. I tried to enjoy the moment, but just felt distress instead. This whole scene felt like a trap, as if something was about to happen. This place was like that—every good thing had its price. One moment you think you're receiving a medical examination, the next you're injected with a substance that turns your leg black and blue. I tried to push away the intrusive thoughts and focus on the music.

"*Langsamer.*" The doctor ordered me to slow down.

His sudden remark startled me, as it was the first word he said to me. I took his order and started playing slower. He was pleased and closed his eyes. Then his violin started speeding up a little and I anxiously tried to play a little faster to match his instrument. He played even faster, and I joined in, rushing my fingers through the music until he abruptly opened his eyes and stopped playing.

"You sped up!" he yelled, and I fearfully stopped too. Was this going to be one of those moments the girls had been talking about, where he would get angry at me? I stared him in the eyes, too afraid to look away.

"It's alright," he tried to comfort me when he saw the fear in my eyes. "You seem tense. Let's take a break, shall we?"

I didn't know how to respond or if I should thank him. He walked me outside the music room and handed me over to another officer. I tried to listen to what they were saying, though they were clearly trying to hide something from me with their quiet chatter.

The officer guided me into another room and asked me to wait inside until he came back. I was standing in the cold, empty space. It was below ten degrees outside, and the room didn't have any heating. I didn't dare move, though it had probably been more than half an hour and no one had come to see me. My legs were starting to hurt, but I didn't want to sit, as the floor felt ice-cold. I looked at my bare feet, which started turning yellow, and I tried to wiggle my toes. Had they forgotten me?

Finally, I could hear someone approaching. There was a sound of a dog barking outside. The door opened. It was dark and I barely saw who it was. The man crouched down and started unleashing the German Shepherd by his side.

Oh god, no.

My body felt too weak to run away, even when hearing the dog growling, as if he was waiting to feast on my flesh.

The man released the dog, which came running at me. I tried to move away, running in circles, but the dog was too quick. He bit my leg. It hurt ten times more than the freezing cold. My legs didn't run as quickly as I wanted them to—my toes were still frozen. With difficulty, I tried to get on top of the windowsill, but as I tried to pull myself up, the dog grabbed my foot. I screamed in pain; the officers laughed. I hadn't seen them all arrive but could hear multiple voices. They were enjoying the show. It probably just seemed like a bullfight to them. I was the bull, and the dog was the man—only, I didn't have the strength to protect myself. I screamed in pain, shouting at the dog to release my foot. I fell down onto my back and hurt my tailbone, but at least the dog let go of my foot. The dog tried grabbing other parts of my body, and I curled up in a small ball, trying to save my limbs. He barked loudly, and I put my hands over my ears. He bit my waist, and I gave out a piercing cry.

Barking, laughter, barking, laughter.

"Stop!" I shrieked.

The dog let go and stepped away. I heard the men approaching but was still curled up on the floor and couldn't see what was happening. I was scared to turn around and have the dog bite my face. There was a burning pain in my wounds. I didn't want to see the blood or ripped flesh.

The man closest to me was holding a gun. I heard the charging handle being lifted.

"Get up," the man ordered. I didn't dare to. "Get up or I shoot," he repeated, louder this time. I slowly tried to push myself up. I remembered the moment when Feline had told me that she wanted the officer to shoot her. For a brief second, I imagined that it would solve all my problems. I wouldn't have to get up and feel the shame or see my wounds. I wouldn't have to endure the pain or live in fear.

But that thought wasn't worth it. I knew I had to survive and get out of this hell of a place, to go back to Amsterdam and see Betty again. To hold her tight and to become the mother she deserved. I thought of how overjoyed I would be to have Betty and Nico, to finally be able to live as a happy family, and to see Ab again. That life was probably closer than I thought. I just had to keep that longing and live another day.

So, I slowly but surely managed to get up and stand on both my feet. The officers' eyes were scanning my body, going over each bite mark, observing the blood streaming down my leg. The men were fascinated by the dog's ability to inflict so much pain on a worthless human being.

Don't let them win, I thought.

Safety over dignity.

Two doctors and a nurse were standing next to my naked body, lying down on a medical table. But they were not there to disinfect my wounds or keep my frozen toes warm. They were examining the inflicted wounds, as well as the rash, wondering if it was a reaction to the dog's poisonous teeth. I could hear every word they were saying, for they would not anaesthetise me. Not even a single body part seemed worthy of that. Instead, they further opened my wounds, touching them and even ripping parts of my injured skin and flesh. I tried not to make a sound, but I tensed my jaw and bit my tongue every time they touched one of my wounds. Meanwhile, the doctors were still discussing how the officer had inflicted a special poison onto the dog's teeth and trying to find out in what way that would affect my body, again mentioning the rashes on my arms and chest. I didn't tell them that the rashes had been there before.

After an hour of pain and thorough examination, they finally decided that they had seen enough and would wait about a month to see the effects of the wounds on my body. Assumably, they were hoping that the wounds would get heavily infected or that I would perhaps start to become insane and maybe even hallucinate. The dog would have probably been vaccinated, but luckily, I had had the precautionary anti-tetanus syringe five years ago. The doctors exited the room, telling the nurse to dress me and send me away. She helped me get up and kept an eye on the door to see if they were really gone. Once she was sure, she sneakily opened a cupboard and took out a cloth, which she held under water to clean my body. The cloth was lukewarm and felt comforting. She applied iodine to my open wounds, which stung a lot, and told me to get dressed before the doctors came back. I thanked her and, with difficulty, walked out of that room.

Kay was shocked and furious after she found out what had happened to me.

"We need to do something. This is inhumane!"

"These things happen every day. You've seen worse—"

"It angers me when these things happen to those I care about!"

We hadn't even known each other for that long, though I felt a very strong connection to Kay. Her charming energy was engaging, and I found myself delighted by her contagious playfulness.

"I'm still standing," I tried to calm her.

"A standing corpse if they continue this any longer!"

"I'm alive—"

"Barely." Her anger turned into sadness. "I have lost so many people."

I thought that hearing her say that would make me cry. But nothing. Since arriving at the camp last year, I hadn't cried a single tear.

I hugged Kay, even though my skin could almost not bare the tight embrace.

"Show me," she demanded. She was a stubborn woman and reminded me of Ab. I knew she wouldn't accept a no, so I lifted my trousers, exposing only the leg which had been the least injured. Kay lifted the other side and saw the deep bites. She gagged.

"It's my daughter's birthday," I tried to change the subject. "We should celebrate."

Kay opened her mouth in slight shock. She swallowed and stopped herself from bringing up anything else or asking any more questions.

"Yes," she said, defeated. "We should."

Sugar wasn't a thing you often saw in the Bloem household, especially during the war. But for her second birthday, little Beppy received a nice spoonful of sugar. Jochem, one of the older brothers, looked with envy.

"Beppy's only a baby. Why can she have sugar?" he said angrily. It was a Saturday, so the whole family was home together, which often led to quarrels.

"Don't be greedy," his father, Kees answered. Annie had come home from the market and said she would be cooking dinner tonight. She asked if her sister Loes could keep an eye on Beppy.

"I'll do it," her brother Stan answered. "Loes can't even take care of an animal."

"At least I'm not dating one," his sister replied, and he pushed her.

Annie was heating up a pot of water and started peeling potatoes. Father Kees read the newspaper and mother Zilvertje was knitting scarves for her children to have during the cold winter months. She was seven months pregnant with the couple's fifth child (or sixth including Beppy).

Jochem and Stan, the sons of the house, had gone to manual labour school and were now working to provide for the family. The daughters, Annie and Loes, went to housekeeping school. Annie hated every minute there and knew she was destined for something else. She often felt frustrated by the simplicity of her family's daily life. Her father was a clever man, who early in life had started working in plumbing. Just like his father and grandfather before him, he was practical and handy, which from a young age helped him provide for his family. Annie believed her father was capable of much more. He could've even been an architect, had he had the right education and better financial stability. The same was true of Zilvertje, who was a lovely and caring mother, as well as an artistic woman. She loved to keep herself busy with arts and crafts and was truly exceptional at it. Zilvertje had the talent and patience to embroider, knit, sew, and sculpt. Unfortunately, the family was very poor, and they didn't have the time to sit around and contemplate the life that they could've had. Instead, their daughter Annie did that for them.

Dinner was ready. Everyone joined at the table and held hands to say a prayer. Beppy sat on the floor and made noises whilst playing with her toys.

"It looks delicious!" Zilvertje complimented the little food that her daughter had been able to scrape together and cook.

"A nice celebration for Beppy," Stan smiled.

It had always frightened the family—what would happen if people found out. There were many traitors in Amsterdam, and one wrong move could send the whole family to a prison camp in the East. To avoid that, they tried to act as naturally as possible and distance themselves from acquaintances and strangers. All they knew was that Beppy was supposedly a little girl from the Dutch East Indies that Zilvertje and Kees adopted. The story they kept on telling was that they both wanted to adopt for a very long time. Once they found an article about the neglectful foster care in the Dutch colony, they decided to adopt Beppy.

Their oldest son, Jochem, still believed his parents were mad for doing this. They didn't have enough money to feed their own children—why would they add a strange baby inside the house? And there was even another one on the way.

Annie had a different opinion. From the moment she first saw Beppy, she fell in love with the little girl and knew she would do anything in her power to take care of her. Even though she was only a baby, the little girl had a fun and witty attitude. Annie walked, fed, played, washed, and shared a bed with her. Stan secretly liked her too, but was more preoccupied with his girlfriend, Danique. He was so head over heels that she seemed to be the only thing on his mind most days. His parents had told him not to invite her over anymore. They didn't trust the girl and were scared of what might happen if she found out. Stan had told her about the adoptee, so he thought that it was foolish not to let her visit. But Annie knew very well that it wasn't just that. Danique was a nasty person; Stan was just too infatuated to see. She was always rude and catty to the family. Zilvertje hoped that Stan would soon come to his senses and realise who she truly was, but Annie knew better. In a few years, the two would be married; she had no doubt about that.

Their relationship just worked—Danique would constantly complain, Stan ran to satisfy her needs, she would get angry, and he would apologise for things he didn't even do. It was a functioning dynamic in which they both got what they wanted, and it seemed to work perfectly. Stan gets Danique; Danique gets a pushover.

Their other daughter, Loes, on the other hand, was quite indifferent to her new little sister, Beppy. Loes wasn't very quick-witted. Simply put, she was definitely not the sharpest tool in the shed. Annie and Loes often walked to school together, but the sisters rarely had anything to talk about. Girls at her school didn't usually like talking about anything other than gossip and boys, Annie had realised. But her sister didn't even speak about that!

When they finished dinner, the boys left the house to go to the pub. Meanwhile, Loes and Annie cleared the table, and father read the newspaper.

"Have you heard anything from Mrs. L?" Annie asked.

"Inside the house, you can call her Bonneka, dear," her mother explained. "And no, there has been no news."

"How long do you think this will last?"

"I don't think we've seen the worst of it yet."

"Where do you think Beppy's parents are?"

Zilvertje didn't reply. Annie disliked it when her parents kept things from her. Regardless, her mother probably didn't even know herself.

It was nine o'clock in the evening. The house was cold after they turned off the gas fireplace. Annie placed Beppy in bed next to her. She caressed her forehead and sang a lullaby.

"Sleep Beppy, sleep,
Outside, there is a sheep.
A sheep with little white feet,
Who drinks its milk so sweet.
Sleep Beppy, sleep,
Outside, there is a sheep."

Beppy slowly but surely closed her eyes and sighed herself to sleep.

"You'll see your mother very soon."

Annie closed her eyes too and fell into a deep slumber.

SPRING, 1944

THE MEDICAL TABLE was like a game of Russian roulette—
most of us always hoped that the loaded chamber wouldn't align
with the primer percussion that day. And yet, we all knew that the
consequences of missing the bullet could often be riskier than the
lethal shot.

The doctor stood over me, holding a large syringe filled with a
white liquid. When the experiments first started, he would tell me an
excuse, like saying that the liquid was a concentration of vitamins to
help my body receive the correct nutrients it was missing. By now,
the doctors had seen me for long enough and didn't make the effort
of giving me false explanations. They knew that I wasn't a screamer. I
had only done so in the very beginning, but by now, I was quite used
to the pain of the needles, cuts, and rashes. Every time they cut open
one of my body parts or injected me with a painful substance, I would
remind myself of our great doctors in Amsterdam. I had to endure

for just a little longer, and would come back home and run to the hospital. *They would help me get rid of all of these toxins*, I imagined.

Three girls in our room had died that week. All of them had gone in for another examination and never came back. Gina tried to keep us calm, saying that their bodies just gave up and that we had to trust that our own anatomies would keep us protected.

"That's bullshit," Kay told me when we were alone. "I overheard the doctors. They injected those girls with phenol."

The doctor held the syringe up and examined my arm. He firmly rubbed my skin to warm it and tapped a couple of times before abruptly inserting the needle. The liquid burnt in my veins. I bit my inner cheeks and took a deep breath trying not to make a sound. The doctor smiled at me and ordered me to immediately stand up. I did as I was told, feeling light-headed by the substance that was rushing through my body.

The nurse brought me to a clinical bedroom where I could lay down on the bed. It was the third time I had received an injection like this. My arm hurt so much that, once the nurse had closed the door, I groaned in pain. My agony concerned her, and she helped me lay down. She sat on my arm to help distract me from the pain. By now, the pain was rushing to my lower abdomen.

"Why me?" I whispered.

The nurse put her hand on my forehead and shushed me.

"You're one of the lucky ones."

I couldn't remember the last time I had my monthly bleeding and wasn't sure whether this was because of the malnutrition and lack of food or from the experiments. I didn't dare ask questions—I kept my mouth shut. One day, the doctor was in such a terrible mood that he injected another poor woman with a random blood type to see how her body would react. Again, they were playing the game of Russian roulette and, unfortunately, she caught the wrong bullet. She became incredibly ill. The nurses in our block tried to give her medication against the pains and made her drink certain substances to keep her kidneys from failing. The woman had so much difficulty urinating, and it usually came out a reddish colour. She screamed every time she had to go and felt the humiliation until her very last day, when her kidneys completely shut down. She went into shock and died soon after.

The nurse, who was still sitting on my arm, introduced herself as Zofia, a Polish prisoner.

"The bites on your body are healing," she said in broken German.

"Yes, I hope so."

I was holding in my breath, which she noticed.

"The injection won't kill you, but a lack of oxygen might."

"What is it then?"

Zofia looked away.

"What are they putting inside my body?"

"Give it a week, and the pain will be reduced." She stood up and left the room.

Zofia was right. It took a week, but eventually the pains did die down. The doctors wanted to check the effects on my body. Every time I entered one of their rooms and saw the medical table, my head started turning, and I would have a gag reflex. The tables became synonymous with feeling pain and having to spend weeks recovering. I tried to hold my head up high and show no fear. Zofia walked me to the table to lay me down. I made sure to focus on my breathing and slow it down whilst my heartbeat fastened.

The doctors spoke over my naked body. I heard them discussing the X-ray machine as well as the injections. The doctors claimed that my body was too strong—fighting against every dose or injury made.

"Let's take out an ovary."

My eyes widened, and I glanced at Zofia in despair. *Please do something!* I tried to tell her through eye contact. My heart started beating even faster. A doctor ordered Zofia to get me ready. I had told myself not to object, but it went too far. This could kill me.

"The woman is already infertile; I would not waste time removing an ovary," Zofia said. All the doctors turned to her with disbelief. Not at what she had said, but because she interrupted them.

"She looks strong and could help carry the dead. There's not enough men to do it, and the bodies are piling up," Zofia explained. *This wouldn't work*, I thought. *First, they'll take out my ovaries, and then they'd kill us both.* Kay would never know; she hadn't seen me for weeks. Heck, she might even be dead.

"Get the utensils and shut up!" The doctor lost his temper.

"Wait one moment." The other doctor asked the men to discuss something outside the room.

It felt like an hour passed by. My naked body was still on the table, whilst Zofia was getting the room ready for the sterilisation.

"I'm infertile?" I whispered.

She glanced at me without responding. Her eyes confirmed it. People had always judged me for wanting a child during the war, but there was not a single bone in my body filled with regret now.

One of the men came back with a female officer. She grabbed Zofia by the hair and pulled her away.

"Stop!"

I stood up and tried to get them to leave her alone, but she was dragged out of the room.

"Put your uniform back on," the man ordered.

I was led outside by an officer who brought me to another side of the camp. As we walked, I could smell a horrid stench— a pile of bodies on the floor. The pile was massive, and a few male prisoners were dragging each body, one by one, on top of a cart. They ordered me to be on dead body duty with the other men. Without asking another question, I grabbed the arms of a body and carried her carefully onto the cart. My back hurt and my knees felt weak, but the officer was observing me carefully, trying to figure out whether I would be strong enough to do the job. I was much taller than some of the men working, and they were bonier than me. I tried to hold in my breath and avoid looking at the body's faces. I told myself that they were just rotten dolls, nothing more. Finally, the officer got bored and moved away. Zofia had helped me survive another day. I wondered where they had taken her.

I took a hand from the pile of bodies and realised that this one was much heavier than the one before. Instead of looking away, I now turned to face it. It was a girl, and I recognised her from somewhere. I grabbed her arm and tried to lift her up. How could she be so heavy? Finally, I managed to pull her out of the pile, but her arm was still stuck inside. I pulled a little bit harder. Then I remembered who she was—Hilla. The left side of her body was stitched to her sister, Tillie. I dropped the bodies and let out a cry of shock. A male prisoner approached me and told me not to worry.

"Their suffering is over," he whispered. He lifted the bodies and dragged them onto the cart. My hands were shaking as I heard a loud thud of the young girls being thrown onto the cart.

———————————

It was Passover, and I was overjoyed to see Kay again. We hugged each other and held on tightly.

"You don't know how much I needed to see you."

"Me too," she replied.

We hadn't seen each other for over a month and both kept an unspoken agreement that we would avoid talking about what had happened to one another during our time apart. I had been on dead body duty for way too long, and every single day, I prayed not to see Kay laying there. Now I was looking at her, alive and well. It gave me a short surge of joy. I was back.

"How was your holiday, my dear?" she asked in a posh tone.

"Oh, darling it was marvellous. We spent three weeks on a cruise," I responded elegantly.

"Please, tell me more!"

"We had *gremsjelish*[7] in the mornings, matzos with fish cakes for lunch, and matzo ball soup and brined meat for dinner."

"What about dessert?"

"Sometimes almond cake, sometimes date *charoset*[8]—"

"And if you can't choose?"

"Then you have both!"

We laughed. I hadn't realised how much I needed Kay. We joked around for a little longer, until I asked where Gina was.

"They found out that she has been giving us ointments and medicine." We both simultaneously looked down at our arms. The marks of our rashes were still there, but the blisters were gone, all thanks to Gina.

"It's Passover! Let's celebrate, not mourn," I told Kay.

The Jewish holidays were not celebrated in the camp. On the contrary, it seemed to be an opportunity for the officers and guards to make us even more miserable. But I had decided that it would not work anymore. Their last drop had overflown my bucket. I was done being the victim.

I wanted to see Nico again, immerse myself in thoughts of how it used to be.

That evening, we received our nightly bowl of "soup," bread, and margarine. Kay and I sat next to each another.

"When was your first time?" she asked wonderingly.

"My first time . . . ?"

She laughed and I understood what she meant.

"With Nico."

"Your husband . . . Before the wedding?"

I nodded mischievously and Kay seemed amazed.

"I didn't take you for a scarlet," she teased. "When?"

"A lady doesn't kiss and tell."

---

7   *Gremsjelish* are Passover cookies made with matzo crackers, sugar, eggs, oil, raisins, and cinnamon.

8   *Charoset* is a sweet paste made of fruits and nuts, eaten at the Passover seder.

"Oh, piss off," she gently pushed me.

We giggled, though I could see that she genuinely wanted to know.

"One summer day, on a camping trip with friends. It was before we were even engaged."

Kay curiously asked for more details. I thought back of that day in Scheveningen.

We were setting up our tents by the dunes. Nico and I had been seeing each other for six months and things were getting more serious. After an evening of drinking, bonfires, and swimming in the cold sea, we finally retreated to our tents.

"Goodnight, love birds." Selma winked at us before closing her tent. It was cosy, just the two of us. Usually, we would separate the girls and the boys, but as the years went by, we changed it to couples' tents. Nico turned on his small angle-head flashlight. I could still see his sweet face, dimly lit by the light. He slowly moved his head closer to mine, waiting for me to make a move. I got slightly nervous and started speaking.

"Tomorrow we should visit the town centre and go on a little adventure. I assume it's going to be as warm as today, which is good. We should try that cute ice-cream shop I was telling you about."

He slowly moved back and smiled with a slightly worried expression.

"What's wrong?"

"It's just . . ."

Nico stopped himself, and I wasn't sure what he meant by this. *Was he trying to break up with me?*

"We've been going out for a while, and I've met your parents—"

I interrupted his awkward speech. "What does that mean?"

"It means that I love you."

His expression was unreadable.

"Do you?" I asked confusedly.

"Uh . . . yes. I do."

No boy had ever told me he loved me. And certainly not a handsome man like Nico. I almost found it hard to believe him.

"You are the most interesting person I've ever met," he tried to explain himself.

I laughed, fully aware of the fact that I was ruining a romantic moment.

"What's so funny?" Nico winced.

"That I love you too!" For some reason, I couldn't stop laughing. There he was, an incredibly handsome and intelligent man, charmingly telling me that he loved me, and all I could do was laugh. *Keep it together, Hanna!* I thought.

I had always been the tomboy, the girl who hung out with guys and talked to them about other girls they fancied. The one who was respected, the girl that other men were scared to play tennis with, for fear of being defeated. Before Nico, I had only ever been on two dates, and both of them went terribly wrong. I had been kissed once, at a school dance, though I later found out that the boy had kissed a few other girls that night.

Nico, on the other hand, was a man who had always been popular with the ladies, even though he never realised it. His mysterious charms could win over anyone. *Why would a man like that go out with a girl like me?* It was something that kept puzzling me.

"You are honest, compassionate, and smart," Nico said. "I still can't believe we're together."

I pulled him closer to kiss my lips. We were both fools in love, and I adored every second of it. He asked me whether I had ever slept with someone, and I shook my head.

"Have you?"

"No," he answered timidly.

I brushed my fingers through his hair and whispered, "Close your eyes," slowly sliding my hand from his crown all the way down to his lower back. He tensed up but seemed to enjoy my touch as he held my hips and guided them closer to him. My heart flipped. Until now,

I had pretended to know what I was doing, but this was all foreign to me. He held my lower back and pulled me closer whilst playfully touching my lips with his. I could feel his breath becoming heavier. My toes curled, and I realised how much I loved him. This was it, the feeling I had read about in so many books, the image that was printed everywhere. Not just love, but a passion for someone you so deeply cherish. It was tense yet romantic. Strange but oh so exciting. I tried to remember what my girlfriends and I had discussed, how to give a man pleasure. Selma had explained how she would do it. I experimented with Nico and saw what he enjoyed and what felt slightly less good to him. I guided him too. We spoke and laughed and made love. And yet, it wasn't fully what I had expected it to be. It felt like something was missing.

Nico saw my slight concern and told me to relax. He tried out some things. He, too, I imagined, had probably spent time talking to his friends about it. I kissed him and we tried again. This time, I felt more at ease. He smiled, noticing my pleasure, and I saw a slight spark in his eyes.

Afterwards, we held each other. "Thank you," he said.

"What are you thanking me for?"

He caressed my back.

"For making me happy."

I was brought back to reality by Kay's surprise. "Did he really say that?" Kay was amused. "That's so corny!"

"Not the way Nico said it. He has his charming ways!"

"You're just in corny love."

"Okay, you tell me your story then!"

She had a slight look of embarrassment.

"I was sixteen years old. My older sister had a boyfriend. I never realised it back then, but I always wanted what she had. One day, she came home with the guy, Dillon, and I heard them making noises upstairs. I asked Charlotte about it when Dillon had left."

"In your house?" I was surprised.

"My parents were working that day. Charlotte was always a bit of a rebel."

Kay smiled when thinking about her sister.

"Anyway, not too long after, I got a boyfriend too. Because God forbid if I didn't copy my sister's every move."

"Who was the boy?"

"Yakov, an older guy from my school, very handsome, and he definitely knew it. Promiscuous."

I hadn't heard about this side of Kay before.

"It was too easy."

"How so?"

"We had only been a couple for three months, then we did it. It wasn't even pleasurable."

"Would you rather have waited?"

"Not a chance. Back then, I was proud that I could finally tell Charlotte about it."

"How did she react?"

"She told me I should immediately break up with Yakov. And I did."

"Was he sad?"

"He started seeing Olivia Langebroek about a week after. I think he was fine."

She explained how it had been, that one time she did it. I couldn't believe that she had only been sixteen. *What if she would have gotten pregnant?*

"We took it out just in time. Yakov didn't want to take that risk either." I couldn't imagine seeing myself doing it at that age. There were so many other things on my mind back then—the crisis, our family's bankruptcy, moving to a smaller home, leaving school, working at the insurance company. I wondered whether all of that had made me skip a large part of my becoming an adolescent. Before leaving school, I did sometimes experience having jitters over a boy, but that would never go any further.

"Do you regret it?" I asked.

"Oh, Hansje, one thing I have realised from being here is that I don't regret or miss a single second of my teenage years! I used to worry about the most idiotic things," Kay continued. "But I would go back to those days in a heartbeat."

My mind drifted away, and I started thinking about Betty. She was still only a toddler, but it wouldn't take long before she would be a young girl. I imagined her in a school uniform, wearing a backpack, and hopping to school. They could keep me here for years to come. A decade might pass without me seeing my girl, and she wouldn't even remember me. She wouldn't happily dance to the tunes I play on the piano. Thinking about the piano made my stomach turn. Every time I imagined the instrument now, all I could think of was Dr. Mengele's out-of-tune, fast-paced violin. It was never really out of tune when he played, yet, in my mind, the strings made loud screeching noises, and all I could hear were shrieks and barking dogs.

Kay knew what I was thinking about.

"You'll see them soon," she whispered. "Nico, Ab, and Betty."

"Nico . . ." I stopped, and she wonderingly looked at me. "We're in the middle of the men's camp."

Kay could see where I was going with this.

"He must be somewhere in this area. Or someone must have seen him at some point!"

"Are you going to ask every man in Birkenau?"

"Yes. Yes, I am."

SUMMER, 1944

I HAD BEEN SENT OFF to dead body duty again. Kay came as well this time. Though she was thin, she still had enough meat on her bones to look more muscular than most of the others. This was because of the experiments, of course. We were fed more than the average male prisoners. Dead body duty was foul and painful. But I felt more at ease with Kay by my side. I remembered the advice that one of the male prisoners had told me, which was to pretend that the bodies were just mouldy dolls. I told Kay this, who didn't seem too happy with this job. We were helping each other carry them onto the carts. The last time I had done this, the men who were with me already seemed on the verge of collapsing. Therefore, I understood why they needed people like Kay and me. We were good at keeping up appearances—don't gobble down your food; keep your spine straight and shoulders back. I often told Kay to stand tall, which was why we had made a game of it. The better we pretended, the longer they would keep us alive to work.

It was a sunny morning in the camp, yet the sky was clouded by a dusty curtain of black smoke. I, again, tried to avoid looking at the corpses' faces. This time, there was a pile of Polish prisoners. They had been lined up and shot for being traitors to the Nazi's.

"They died with honour," a male prisoner said. He spoke to me in Dutch.

"How so?"

The man came slightly closer, as if to help me carry a body.

"The officers earlier, I overheard them speaking of an uprising in Warsaw."

"I wonder how long it will take until a country will bomb this place."

"Should we bet on it?"

He laughed, helping me pick up another body.

"Soviets."

"Not a chance. USA, I bet," he replied.

"Who is to say it won't be the Brits?" Kay joined our conversation. The bodies were on the cart, and the men were getting ready to carry them to the crematorium. The women had to stay behind, as they wouldn't allow both sexes to socialise without supervision.

"I'm Aron," he introduced himself.

"Hanna," I smiled.

The fact that the man spoke Dutch made me wonder whether he might have met Nico at some point. For months, I had been asking almost every male prisoner I could speak to, but with no result.

"This might be a shot in the dark, but have you met a Dutch man named Nico? He's around my height and a quiet yet very clever man. Dark eyes—"

Aron's face became solemn.

"Hanna," he repeated. "Hansje?"

I stared at him, feeling a mild astonishment. "My nickname."

"Funny, I thought he was exaggerating when he said you were tall." He looked me up and down.

"Do you know my husband, Nico?"

"So, you are Nico's wife!"

My eyes opened widely.

"How is he? Can I see him?"

I felt an anxious sensation of exhilaration, until I saw Aron's expression change. He looked down at his feet and his forehead tensed.

"What?" I asked, but this time my voice dropped.

He raised his gaze and forced a wistful smile. "Hansje, I am truly sorry."

"Don't call me that."

He was lying. I knew he was. There was no way this man knew my husband. He was talking about someone else—I was so sure. There were plenty of Dutch men called Nico. And plenty of women named Hansje. It was too strange to be true. The faces of the corpses began to look blurry. They all resembled Nico. I searched through the piles and pits, praying he was not amongst them. Every single face that I had chosen not to look at could have been him. Now I turned over each corpse and struggled to remember what he looked like.

Aron could see my frustration and grabbed my arm.

"You'll get yourself killed."

The officers came back, ordering us to continue working. I felt angry, and not a single bone in my body wanted to go back to work. I needed to find Nico.

This time, there was a gunshot. Aron gave me a nod and grabbed the cart. Kay gestured that I should go back to the block with her. But instead, I took off my headscarf, hid my face from the officers, and took hold of the cart. I could feel Kay's gaze of concern on me, but I wouldn't be able to go back without getting answers. We began pulling the cart to the crematorium and walked in silence for a couple of minutes. If one of the officers would see me, I'd be in big trouble. They might even shoot me on the spot. I tried to pull as hard as I could. Aron was behind me. He also had a look of concern. Even though I knew I was risking my life, the possibility of never seeing Aron again felt worse. I had to take my chances. The walk was longer than I thought, and my arms felt like they were going to fall off. An officer walked along, pointing his riffle at us for fun, though I knew he wouldn't shoot us. If anything, he would shoot us after we had finished doing our work. The officer did threaten to shoot us whenever we slowed down. The crematorium was a long building, with a tall chimney blowing black dust into the sky. It smelled of coal and burnt flesh.

The officer stayed behind. I realised he was just a coward who couldn't stand the sight of dead bodies. Even when we had been walking, he had not once looked at the cart. Over the years, I realised that a lot of them were just young men trying to prove their authority by scaring us. Still, when I looked into these young officers' eyes, all I could see were frightened little boys.

We finally arrived at the crematorium and left the cart to the *Sonderkommando*[9,] who would throw the bodies into the ovens. I grabbed Aron's shirt and pulled him behind a wall, out of sight of the other prisoners.

"What happened to Nico?"

"Last winter," Aron was finding it difficult to make a sentence.

"How?" I asked. I had to make sure he was wrong.

"Your husband should have never been assigned to the construction Kommando."

Aron was trying to find the right words to explain it.

"Just tell me everything, I want to know how my husband died."

"I'm not sure if I should."

"I can take it."

Whether I could or not wasn't important. I needed to hear the full story to know if it was true. The only thing that mattered was

---

9   The *Sonderkommando* is a work unit made up of Nazi death camps prisoners, whose job it was to dispose of the corpses at the cremation sites.

that I could hear about a time when Nico was alive. His last moments were the only ones I could hold on to.

"Tell me everything."

He sighed deeply.

"A group of us were sent to another camp."

"What kind of camp?"

In my mind, there were only two camps—Auschwitz, which was where we were in September, and Birkenau, which was where we were now.

"It's called Buna. And believe me, this camp is a walk in the park compared to that place."

"Buna. I haven't heard that name before."

"They changed the name just before I left. Now it's called Arbeitslager Monowitz, I think," Aron's voice dropped.

"Was he gassed?" I bit my lip.

"No. Fortunately not."

I wasn't sure if I would've gone as far as to use the word *fortunately*.

"How, then?"

We were trying to whisper, but others had started noticing our presence. If I had learnt anything, it was that there were snitches everywhere, so we had to get out before someone would call an officer. We got out of the crematorium and went outside where a group of officers were staring at us. They saw my face, and I froze.

One of them came closer and grabbed my shoulder. He took out a gun and pointed it at my temple.

"*Geh zurück in deine Kaserne, Schwein!*"

Aron clearly didn't understand German, as he went down on his knees.

His body was tensing up.

The officer pushed me.

"*Ja, Offizier,*" I replied in a very low voice. I grabbed Aron and pulled him up. We quickly walked past them. Aron was about to turn his head back.

"Don't look at them," I said under my breath. "I've seen this happen before. If you look, they shoot. Just walk."

We finally got out of the officer's sight, and I let out a deep sigh. For once, I felt happy to look like a man.

When we got closer to our block, Aron gestured that I should follow him. He took me behind one of the buildings where the corners were overshadowed with another wall so that this obvious path became a blind spot to any passers-by.

"This will be safe for another hour," he said. "Until the sun moves further east."

We sat down with our backs to the wall, and my heartbeat finally slowed down. The tension made me forget about Nico for a minute.

"He died of exhaustion."

My mind almost couldn't comprehend what Aron was telling me. It had been so long since I last saw Nico. And I was so exhausted that it even became difficult to picture his face.

"In the middle of October last year, you remember how cold it was. We had to stand outside with our bare feet in the mud, waiting whilst the SS men were selecting who would go to Buna. Nico and I were some of the unlucky ones. We had to get into the open lorries with our bare feet in the freezing cold. It was difficult, for Nico especially."

I remembered my first few weeks at the camp, having to wait in the cold, that night when Feline had to run around naked. It hurt me to think of Nico feeling this way.

Aron continued, "We immediately had to go to work, with no food."

"What kind of work?" I asked.

"A load of bollocks, that's what it was. Carrying iron bars and sacks of cement, unloading heavy ovens. It was a massive factory, IG Farben."

I didn't look at Aron.

"In December, Nico had already lost half of his body weight . . ."

Aron stopped himself.

"Go on."

"Are you sure?"

I nodded, gazing ahead to avoid his eyes.

"He was carrying a fifty-kilogram sack of stones up a flight of stairs. They were beating him. I tried to help—I swear! But they were beating me too."

His voice quivered.

"It's okay," I tried to reassure Aron. "Thank you for wanting to help him."

"Next thing I knew, his body was on a cart, and I was in a lorry on the way to the gas chambers."

"How are you still here then?"

"Because I was in the *Sonderkommando,* and I have been working at Birkenau ever since."

From a distance, I could see Dr. Mengele shouting at some of his assistants. A couple of officers trod carefully to approach the madman, which only seemed to intensify his rage.

"Don't look," Aron insisted.

"Why?"

"You'll get caught!"

The man was so focused on his temper tantrum that he had no eyes for anyone else. The assistant and the other officers were also silently standing there, trying to divulge his attention. A look of concern flashed over their faces as the doctor finally mumbled his last words. His red face turned pale. "*Wir sind verloren.*"

Aron grabbed my arm.

"Stop looking!"

For a brief moment, I had the urge to take advantage of this disempowerment by getting up and provoking all the other prisoners to revolt. Aron clasped my arm, and I took a deep breath in. "They are losing the war."

He released my arm.

"They haven't lost just yet."

———————————

During the early morning roll call, Dr. Mengele appeared behind a group of prisoners who were being sent to a different camp. As he approached, I inhaled his familiar chemical smell, which reminded me of a hospital bedroom.

The women were softly sobbing as he ordered an officer to load them onto a truck and bring them to the showers. He turned around and scanned us women, standing still and waiting for the officers to call out our numbers. The doctor pointed at a young girl who was standing opposite me. "She also needs a shower."

The girl fell to her knees and begged the officers not to take her. I bit the insides of my cheeks whilst the doctor turned his head to look over his shoulder. We clocked eyes.

"Schubert," he smiled. His gaze moved down to my legs. "How are your dog bites?"

I swallowed. By now, I could feel the scars in my inner cheeks as he lifted his finger to point at me.

"This woman is a virtuoso on the clavier," he said to the other officers. I wasn't even sure whether he still remembered the incident with the dog last winter.

"How are your bites?"

So, he did.

"Don't be shy." He smiled again.

"They are better. Thank you."

His smile widened, and he ordered the officers to transport the women. I was released from roll call and had to follow the doctor to his music room. Not a single bone in my body was ready to play again.

"Virtuoso," he muttered so quietly. I wasn't sure whether that was the exact word he used. "I am in dire need of some relaxation. Play any tune that you love." And so, I did as I was told. The first tune was a melody that I knew he was fond of. He would often hum it when he was in a good mood.

"No. A tune that *you* love."

There was one song that had been stuck in my head for a while. It was a song that I heard in my dreams, though I didn't know the right chords.

First, I softly hummed a line.

"Sleep Baby, sleep . . ."

And matched the right chords to the tune.

"Outside, there is a sheep . . ."

I found the notes to play the tune which had been stuck in my head for so long. A melody of a children's lullaby. I looped the song a few times, and the doctor closed his eyes.

"This is beautiful, Virtuoso. Thank you."

There was a genuine gratefulness in his voice. The authenticity of his voice reminded me that he was just a person—someone who, like anyone else, had once been a child. I imagined the doctor as a child, with fear in his eyes, and I finally felt a sense of control again. They were losing the war, and this man was afraid for his life. Now he was surrendering to what was yet to come, and I just had to wait. Just a little longer.

WINTER, LATE 1944

IT WAS SEVEN IN THE EVENING, and the last stump of candle at the Bloem family's house was burning out. Zilvertje had managed to get some watery stew from the central soup kitchen. She had stood in line for hours, only to gather half a pot of food, which would have to fill all of them up for the next twenty hours.

"Send the little ones away," Kees kept telling his wife. "This famine will be the death of them!"

"We cannot risk it."

"Beppy will be fine. All anyone is concerned about nowadays is getting food on their plates." Their son Jochem was even more angry these days.

The winter was hard. Not only was there a crisp cold and piercing wind in the air, but the coal supply had been stopped, making the living conditions even more unbearable. Fuel, or lack thereof, kept the houses frigid and the people bitter. But the worst of it was the food shortage. The Bloem's family hadn't been properly fed in months, and it was starting to show in their miserable family dynamic. At first, their eldest son, Stan, blamed it on the government trying to preserve their stock for the rich, but soon, they had found out that everyone was starving, even those with money. Bread was worth ten times more than gold.

The family finished their cold stew and went to bed before the candle burnt out. Zilvertje cried herself to sleep, not knowing how to keep her family alive. She had two toddlers in her house and had grown so fond of little Beppy—she considered her to be part of the family. And yet, Zilvertje found it difficult to have to feed another mouth. The little girl did not eat much, but every little crumb she ate was one taken from another child. She thought of what to do. Some children were evacuated to the countryside, where food was still being cultivated. They would have to work for the farmer families, and in return, they would receive some of it on their plates. It felt like a plausible solution, though she realised that her children would never want to leave. Kees heard his wife's sobs and turned around. "Don't waste your bodily liquids on useless contemplations."

"There's less and less every day. What if Beppy doesn't survive?"

"What if we don't?"

"We've made a promise to her mother."

"If we're starving, then Beppy's mother probably is too."

"We have to do something!" Her husband's squabbling incompetence angered her.

"I don't know what it is that you want me to do," he admitted.

"I would like to see you queue at the soup kitchen until your toes freeze off."

"I have to work!"

"For what? What money do we need when we can't even buy an ounce of cheese?"

"Alright, I'll go to the soup kitchen tomorrow, and you can stay home and complain some more."

His passive aggressiveness was making Zilvertje more and more frustrated.

"Or better yet," she replied, "you will stay home to take care of the children. Send Annie and Loes to find food, and Jochem and Stan can work."

"Whilst you do what exactly?"

"Some women are cycling to the east of the country to find food and shelter. I know that Liselotte is leaving tomorrow. Perhaps I can join her?" Zilvertje could not see her husband's face in the dark and wasn't sure what his reaction was.

After a couple of seconds of silence, Kees said, "That is far too dangerous."

She realised that the idea sounded quite absurd at first thought. She rarely left her area, let alone the city. But it was a risk she would have to take.

"I don't want you begging like those other food hunters," he said.

"No need to beg if we can scrape together our silver cutlery, my embroidery, some clothes, or textiles. I'm sure they will take any payment."

"How long will you be gone?" This time, he revealed his genuine concern, which made her reconsider whether this was a good idea—though she still thought that there was no other choice.

"This way, we'll have enough to last us the next few months. The winter is getting colder, and I'm afraid that the rations will only get scarcer."

She caressed his cheek and noticed his heavy breathing.

"Our children are brave, and I will only be gone for a couple of weeks."

"Fine," Kees sighed. "But you're the one telling them this tomorrow."

That thought kept her eyes wide open until the morning sun.

———

A part of me still longed for Nico's touch. Nevertheless, I had been spending more time with Aron, searching for his company. Whenever we spent time alone, he rarely mentioned Nico, knowing that I still referred to him as a living man, my living husband, working somewhere in another concentration camp. I trusted Aron, since we had been getting closer, and yet a part of me liked to believe that he didn't know the whole truth. Perhaps the fatigue had made him delusional.

It was a Sunday afternoon.

We sat opposite the unloading ramp, hiding behind our usual corner. Not only was it the perfect blind spot, but it was also close to a gravel path, so whenever a person approached, we could hear from afar, giving us plenty of time to hide.

"How is Kay?" Aron smiled.

She had been in pain for the past few weeks. There was a huge cut close to her uterus, closed with stitches which barely held her skin together. It made the other parts of her abdomen black and blue, and there was puss coming out of the stitches. She had been losing patches of hair; now her head was covered in bald spots. She was still struggling with the occasional fever, and even though her abdominal wounds were healing, the pain still seemed excruciatingly fresh.

"Kay is good."

Aron offered me a piece of black bread, and I hungrily took a bite of it. We hadn't kissed or rarely even held hands—it felt like too much of a betrayal. Aron and I were just friends, though Kay always suggested otherwise.

Once I had finished the bread, Aron lowered his chin as if he was looking for approval to come closer. I did not accept or deny, so he leaned forward and kissed my shoulder. I didn't look at him but gently lowered the corners of my mouth. Aron looked at my fingers and noticed the bruises on my hands.

"Have you been playing?" he voiced his concern.

"The doctor asks me once a day."

"I see you haven't given him the perfection he desires."

"He's not as unkind as you might think!"

Aron rolled his eyes, unimpressed by my unnecessary defence. I turned away.

"I would love to hear you play," he whispered.

"One day," I stood up and left, though I could feel Aron's gaze on me as I walked away. Even though he was thinner, paler, and seemingly fatigued, he still treated me as a lady who needed his protection. I enjoyed our conversations and his attention, but still wanted to keep our meetings short and not give him the wrong idea.

I had kept a small piece of the bread for Kay, which I gave her later that evening. She ate it whilst I took out the tube of ointment from underneath the bed. We were running out and the nurses had not been giving us supplies for months now, so I squeezed out as much as I could and applied it to Kay's abdomen.

"How's your sweetheart?"

"Don't call him that," I shushed her. "He told me some interesting news today."

Kay lowered her voice to match my secretive tone.

"Did it involve a ring?"

I ignored her comment.

"He has been getting close to a Slovak gentleman, a gentile of the resistance who got captured last summer."

Aron had been a teacher and was a big history and geography nerd, both subjects he taught. So, he spent a lot of time speaking to prisoners of war. They appreciated his awe and enjoyed discussing the intellectual matters of their actions with someone who actually cared to listen. I wasn't always as interested when Aron tried to explain to me their victories and defeats, but this time, something different caught my attention. Aron told me a rumour, which he heard from the Slovak.

"What is it then?" Kay could not hide her curiosity.

"Apparently, he claims that the Soviets are nearing Auschwitz." She gasped, and I pressed my hand on her mouth.

"It's true," another woman had overheard our conversation. She spoke to us in German but had probably understood the words *Soviets* and *Auschwitz.*

Others sleeping next to us became curious now too. I decided to keep my mouth shut, as I did not want to be known as the one who came up with the rumour. They all were whispering, asking what had been said. The other woman explained it to most of them, and it went in a chain to almost everyone in the barrack.

"Are you sure about this?" Kay tried to be quiet.

I shook my head.

There was unspoken hankering for freedom in the barrack.

"And even if it were true, that doesn't necessarily mean we'll be free." Kay knew I was right. We had to keep our heads low.

But before we knew it, the rumour had made its way around the whole camp. The thing under everyone's breaths. *Liberation.*

Annie had been told not to open the door for strangers. She hadn't seen her mother for almost a week and was home alone when she heard a knock on the front door. It sounded less ominous than that of a Gestapo officer, but more urgent than a neighbour asking for sugar, though that would be a rarity these days. Annie decided to open the door ajar and noticed a blond woman with a friendly face.

"You must be Annie," she said. "I've heard you've been taking care of your new little sister."

Annie was surprised that the woman knew her name. She opened her bag and discretely took out a loaf of bread. "For your family," she said.

Even though Annie wasn't sure whether she could trust her, a gut feeling told her to let the woman in.

"Thank you. I wish I could offer you some tea," Annie admitted. Beppy was playing on the floor and the woman looked at her lovingly. "You've taken good care of her," she said without taking her eyes off Beppy.

Annie was holding the loaf of bread and its smell enriched her nostrils.

All she wanted to do was take a bite.

"It is a token of gratitude."

Annie wasn't sure what to say. Her mother always instructed her to listen when grown-ups were speaking and only respond if required.

"My parents aren't home," Annie responded urgently. She wondered whether the woman was here to take Beppy away.

"I wouldn't normally visit, but there are some urgent matters, and I can't stay for long."

She put her hand out. "You've probably heard of me, I'm auntie Bonneka. Can you safely inform your parents of what I am about to tell you?"

Annie was only half listening, too distracted by the bread in her hand, though she nodded.

"I know Beppy's mother. She's a good friend of mine. But do not repeat that to anyone other than your parents! Do you understand?"

Annie nodded again.

"The hunger is dreadful, but at least the people are preoccupied with something far more important. I will try to come back each week to bring you some more food. I don't normally do this, but your little sister holds a dear place in my heart."

Auntie Bonneka was about to leave.

"How is she?" Annie stopped her. "Beppy's mother."

Bonneka turned around and raised an eyebrow: "You're a clever girl. I can sense it."

She smiled and took one step closer to Annie, yet still doubtfully keeping her voice low.

"I just want to know if she's alright, that's all."

"I don't know where her mother is, and that is the truth," Bonneka sighed. "But that is our secret."

Annie nodded, unsatisfied with her response.

"Another piece of advice. From now on, don't let strangers get inside when your parents aren't home," Bonneka closed the door behind her.

Annie stood still. Beppy was still playing with her toys, giggling.

"Don't laugh at me. She bribed me with bread!"

"Bo-ne-ka."

Annie clapped enthusiastically, "Yes, well done, Beppie! That's Bonneka!"

———————————

I was playing the piano with Dr. Mengele, until we got interrupted by a few officers. They told him to urgently go with them; without turning an eye, he left me at the piano. My head felt heavy, and I softly closed my eyes for a few minutes. *Just a quick nap*, I thought. *I would definitely wake up before he returns.*

When I woke up, my head was resting on the piano keys, and I got a quick fright, hoping no one had heard me make sounds.

No one seemed to be nearby, and I was waiting for another long while. My fingers began touching different keys, one by one, creating a recognisable tune. They remembered the motions which produced "Für Elise," a song I hadn't played since that evening at Mrs. Nijsens' house. I hadn't heard of or seen her since and didn't even fully remember what she looked like. The images of our time at her house were a blur, and the song just brought back a distant memory, nothing more. I wasn't even sure whether Betty even liked this song—did I play it for her? It all felt so far away. Another life.

The doctor still wasn't back. I must have been there for at least three hours, and he might have forgotten about me. So, I got up, closed the piano, and left the room. My stomach was rumbling, and when I noticed it was already dark outside, I was hoping I hadn't missed dinner, though I had not been able to eat much in the last few days, feeling quite light-headed.

When I got outside, I recognised Aron's voice.

He ran towards me and grabbed both my shoulders. He seemed surprised and hugged me tightly, though I could not return the affection.

"Thank God!"

"What's wrong?" My throat was sore.

"Kay said she couldn't find you, so I've been looking everywhere. I was so scared they had taken you!"

Aron guided me to our usual spot, though I was still processing what he was telling me.

"That they took me?" I asked.

"You were gone for so long. They've been rounding up prisoners to leave the camps, but we don't know where to."

"Here?"

"In Auschwitz."

He kissed my cheek. I told him I had been playing the piano, so I wasn't aware of what was going on.

"How long have you been playing?" he asked.

"A couple of hours," I said, though I wasn't sure.

"Hanna, you've been gone almost two days!"

He was being ridiculous. I napped for a little whilst I was waiting for Dr. Mengele to come back, but I hadn't been there that long.

"Did you fall asleep?"

"I might have closed my eyes for five minutes."

"Oh, God, you must be starving!" His hysteria was making me anxious, so I told him I wasn't hungry, even though the thought of food made my mouth water.

"So, people have been sent away?"

He confirmed that some groups had, but that he didn't know anything about what was happening.

"We need to stay together," he said. But all I could think about was finding Kay.

"After the Soviets come to free us, and when we get back to Amsterdam, I can't wait to meet Betty," Aron whispered.

His words were kind, though I did not remember telling him about having a daughter, let alone mentioning her name.

"Nico told me."

It all felt ridiculous. I wasn't even sure whether Nico was dead, and another man was already talking about meeting my daughter. I was avoiding looking into Aron's eyes and shifted my gaze.

"Did I go too far?" he stuttered.

"No," I said with a false smile.

He kissed me on the lips, and I defenselessly stood still.

"A kiss for good luck," Aron said.

His words made me shudder and I couldn't say a thing. Aron saw my concern. "That's what Nico used to say to you."

I leaned back.

"You can't say that . . ." My lips were trembling as I felt the blood rushing through my veins.

"Hanna, you have been the only good thing about this place," he stuttered. "But I know that I will never be him."

I bit my tongue and stood up.

"Goodbye, Aron," I said.

Aron's face went white. "I'm sorry, I shouldn't have . . ."

Without looking back, I began to walk away. My body felt numb. Aron knew Nico. And Nico was dead. There was no denying it anymore. All I could think of were his last moments, how he had been struggling. An image of a thin and pale Nico, coughing in the bitter cold. My hands felt clammy as I passed the other officers and prisoners, holding my head up high with a straight face. Not to show any sign of weakness.

I had to hold my nose whilst entering the barracks. The smells had become unbearable. Half of the girls had disappeared, and though the extra sleeping space felt comforting, the sudden emptiness was concerning.

Luckily, Kay was there. She had patiently been waiting for my return, knowing that I would find my way back to her. I didn't mention what I had been doing for the past two days.

It was incredibly cold, but I was more preoccupied with my dizziness and headache.

Even though I had rejected Aron, I still craved the comfort and warmth he could give me. Regardless, the person who I longed for the most was Nico. There was still a little voice in the back of my head whispering that he could be alive. That Aron had not seen him wake up.

Kay was spooning me, her hands feeling incredibly cold, too, so I rubbed them with mine.

"Nico is dead."

"I know, Hanna," she said.

"He can't be . . ."

I felt stupid. *I had been too hopeful*, I thought. Now there was this heaviness in my chest.

"Sleep," she said, but I couldn't close an eye that entire night.

WINTER, EARLY 1945

THEY WOKE US UP earlier than usual, and this time there was no
roll call. We had to get into a line and follow the officers.

"No eating until we arrive!"

I didn't understand what was happening and held onto Kay. She
looked at me with disbelief and stared at our bare feet.

"We're going somewhere to work," a girl next to us explained.
"The guard told me."

"Enough! Enough!" a woman in front of the line cried. But before
the other could shush the woman, an officer had already shot her,
and she helplessly fell to a quick death. I tried to keep my head low
not show myself to the guards.

"We need to go back," Kay said, pointing at our bare feet, walking
through the snow.

"Are you mad?"

"Trust me!"

We ducked down and passed through the hoard of women. Kay counted to three and we entered one of the garrisons. There were beds and a few latrines, but it was mostly empty. I found a couple of blankets underneath one of the beds. Someone must have hid them, though there was no time to contemplate, so I quickly took the blankets, rolled them up, and hid them underneath my shirt.

Kay triumphantly showed me two pairs of men's shoes.

"Where did you find them?"

"You don't want to know."

She threw me a pair, which I quickly put on, and I gave her one of the blankets. We hurried through the corridor. The front door was still open, and we stealthily got back into the moving crowd. No one had noticed us.

"Where is Aron?"

I was looking behind me, but there were only women. Kay grabbed my arm and pulled me towards her.

"Don't get yourself shot."

We passed the exit of Birkenau, and that's when I realised it would be the last time I'd ever see this place. There was snow and a deadly silence. I was grateful for the shoes. Some of the women had to walk on their bare feet. The blanket helped keep me warmer, though I could still feel the piercing cold through my whole body. My headscarf was too thin to keep my ears warm, and I heard my heartbeat in my eardrums.

They kept on guiding us through the snow. We marched, still in silence.

There was no landscape to be seen through the mist.

Kay stared into the distance with terror in her eyes.

"They are going to kill us," she said softly so no one could hear, not that anyone was listening. The faces of all these malnourished women were staring into nothingness.

"They wouldn't go through all this effort. If they wanted to kill us, we'd already be dead."

She shook her head.

"You're a tiger," I whispered. "Tigers fight."

She held her stomach. The infection was gone, though I could tell that she still felt a stinging pain near her scars.

"I won't have children," she said hopelessly.

"We are being sent somewhere to work. You heard it yourself." Her lips were trembling, her cheeks looking red and swollen.

"Work that will be the death of us."

I refused to believe that.

I tried to tread the snow as lightly as possible, though my toes were burning and my whole body felt like collapsing at any moment.

I had almost died many times by now, but in this moment, it was closer than it had ever felt. I could just fall down, and the pain would be gone. I was sure Kay was thinking the same thing. A woman in front of us was walking slower, and we had to pass her. She truly tried to keep up, though after what felt like an hour, the woman gave up. I heard the sound of a shot behind me but kept looking forward. If I did not face death, then I would not see it as an option. Kay and I were holding hands, though I could barely feel it anymore. The senses in my fingertips had disappeared. I felt a burning sensation whenever I tried to warm them.

I looked at all those around me, lifeless creatures marching through the snow in pyjamas. Kay always had something to say, but now she was silent. I had this intense urge to somehow make her smile.

At least Nico didn't have to endure this. He was safe. Aron wasn't. I was too caught up with Nico's death that I failed to think about Aron's kindness. Had he been good-natured, or had he been taking advantage of my grief? Did I say goodbye too soon? Should I have allowed myself the warmth of his embrace?

Kay softly squeezed my hand, as though she could read my thoughts. She gently touched my frozen fingers with the tip of her thumb, trying to warm them up.

I looked her in the eyes, nodded, and smiled. There were so many things I wanted to tell her. So many words in my mind. But all I could do was hold her hand tightly and show that I was there for her. Nevertheless, doubt overtook my face. I tried to look away—to hide my thoughts. I realised I did not want Aron. He would never be Nico. I only wanted Nico.

Another girl collapsed behind me, and I heard the shot close behind me. It was as if it were merely one step away.

My mouth was so dry that I could not taste my cracked lips anymore. The snow looked so incredibly succulent. I slowly crouched down to grab a handful. The snow in my hand started melting, and I immediately shoved some inside my mouth, trying to savour each drop. The cold frosted my lips, though it didn't matter to me. I wanted to crouch down for more but was scared of being shot, so I kept myself straight up and kept my mouth open, trying to catch some of the falling snowflakes.

As we walked, I could see the sun setting.

———————

Auntie Bonneka had done as promised. Though she rarely entered the Bloem family's home, she left a basket with food every two weeks or whenever she could get her hand on something fresh.

Zilvertje, who had successfully returned from her trip with two full bags of potatoes and a whole chicken, was delighted by the abundance of food in her home. It was not as much as they normally ate, but at least the family was not starving, unlike other families in the city. Most little kids or even toddlers were met with a worse fate. And there was nothing they could do about it.

"The war has to end soon!" Kees was getting more and more frustrated.

"And it will." His wife tried to comfort him.

There was a knock on the door. It sounded like Auntie Bonneka.

"We should let her in," Zilvertje said.

"It is too dangerous!"

"There are surely more important things on our neighbour's minds." Zilvertje went to open the door.

"I'm so sorry," Bonneka said. "I only managed to bring apples this time."

"No need to apologise! It is more than enough, truly. Would you like to come in?"

"Oh, no, I shouldn't . . ."

"Please do!"

Bonneka finally accepted their offer and walked inside.

"Bonneka, isn't it?" Zilvertje asked.

"That is what everyone calls me."

"What shall we call you?"

"Bonneka or Mrs. L will do."

"Very well," Kees joined the conversation. He took off his hat and nodded to the stranger in his house.

"I've never been one for small talk," Bonneka admitted.

"When there is war and starvation, small talk seems to be the only escape to normality," Zilvertje smiled.

They chatted for a few minutes, though Zilvertje could sense that Bonneka felt uncomfortable.

Meanwhile, Stan, who had lied about going to the soup kitchen, was in the south of Amsterdam biking with his girlfriend, Danique.

"I have not seen your parents in a long time," Danique said with slight irritation.

"You will soon," Stan lied.

"Do they not want to see me?"

"Of course, they do," Stan said unconvincingly.

"Then why can I not come to your house? I understood last year that they felt embarrassed about the lack of food in your house, but now everyone is starving! No need to be ashamed."

Stan didn't respond.

"So, are we going to your house?"

"I would much rather be alone with you."

"And I would much rather be somewhere warm and cosy. It's freezing outside!"

"You know how my mother is. We can't just surprise her like that."

"Who is more important? Your mother or your future wife?"

She stopped her bike and crossed her arms, which took Stan by surprise, so he held his brakes.

"Why did you stop?"

"Who is more important?"

"You, of course!" he immediately predicated.

"Then let's go to your house."

"Alright," he said, lowering his head.

Danique got off her bike and lifted his chin to kiss him.

"I'm sure they'll be delighted to see me."

Jochem slammed open the front door and stepped inside the living room. "Darling, you're back! Say hello to . . ." Before Zilvertje could finish her sentence, Jochem went into the girls' room. He came back out holding Beppy.

"What are you doing? She was sleeping!" Jochem didn't react to his mother and put the little girl in her pram. Her clueless eyes were only half open, succumbing her to a yawn. "I'm taking her to the park. I'll explain later." Zilvertje stood up, trying to comprehend her son's sudden rush to leave with Beppy. A tense silence filled the room until a couple of moments later when the front door was opened again.

This time, it was Stan and Danique who were standing at the doorway. Bonneka froze when she saw the girl with the long blond hair and freckles.

"Bonneka Leysen!" Danique voiced loudly.

"Danique, how are you, darling?" Bonneka tried to force a smile. She glared at Zilvertje with a hidden frown.

"Her husband and my dad work together," Danique said to Stan. "What a coincidence! I must tell father."

"That won't be necessary. I'm just chatting to my old friend, Mrs. Bloem."

Bonneka quickly grabbed her things, kissed the family goodbye, and left in a hurry.

Zilvertje took a deep breath. "Danique, how good to see you," she said calmly.

"I must see my family-in-law more often. So, I was thrilled when Stan asked me to come in to say hi."

Now Zilvertje understood why Jochem had taken Beppy to the park.

"Well, as much as I would love for you to stay, Stan should really get to the soup kitchen before it's too late," she said.

"Stan, you didn't tell me you had to go to the soup kitchen. How foolish of you! Now you're making me look bad." Danique rolled her eyes.

"I'm going now," Stan said, one foot out the door.

"Lovely seeing you, Danique. Do let us know before you come next time, so we can make sure to have the house heated." Zilvertje closed the door behind them.

Kees sighed and collapsed onto the couch.

"I do not trust that girl one bit," Zilvertje spat. "Imagine if Beppy would've been home."

"It's fine. Nothing happened."

"Well, she saw Bonneka . . ."

". . . who could easily just be a friend of the family."

"At least Jochem caught them soon enough. He's finally showing some responsibility."

"And there's one thing Danique is right about," Kees laughed. "Stan is a fool."

Jochem was walking the pram and looked at the little girl who was silently sleeping. He couldn't help but feel a sense of protectiveness over her. She was so small and helpless. For so long, he had tried to resist looking into the little girl's eyes, but now he longed for her to open them.

———————————

I had seen two more sunsets. We were still walking. I wasn't sure what time of day it was when we finally arrived at a railroad, and I felt incredibly joyful to see the tracks. The guards quickly shoved us inside coal transporters, which had no roof. Kay and I sat in a corner, wrapped in our blankets. I watched the others shiver in their ripped pyjamas as I tightly held onto my blanket.

After a few hours, the train arrived at a station. There were people—actual civilians—who wore normal clothes and, though still quite thin, seemed to be less malnourished than all of us. Kay and I looked at one another, our eyes glimmering. We hadn't exchanged a word for days, but we still managed to communicate and understand one another. I knew what we were both thinking—are they going to let us back into normal society?

We got out of the train and saw a group of women behind the fence, holding bread and jugs of water. My mouth watered at the thought of gulping it down. The women were waving, as if trying to explain that the food was for us, though the guards were guiding us in a different direction. I looked at all the prisoners in front of me and saw that they were leading them into a different train. Were they going to send us back? The women were so desperate to give us food that they ran towards an overpass and threw some of it through the barricade of guards.

We were too tired to protest the guards, and so they led us into the new train, ignoring the women who were trying to feed us.

"*Musí jíst, prosím!*" a woman shouted.

The train left the station, and I thought about the words the woman had used.

"*Prosím,*" I finally repeated with a hoarse voice. It surprised Kay to hear me speak. I was almost certain that I knew what it meant, but I had to be sure.

Prosím was what Bonneka always said. She used that word for so many things—please, you're welcome, hello, good day . . .

Kay murmured a sound. A look of puzzlement crossed her face. "*Prosím*. A woman shouted it. But it's not Polish. It's Czech."

Kay's eyes widened. She didn't reply, but there was sharpness in her silence. She understood what that meant. We looked at one another with bewilderment. We were not in Poland anymore. This was Czechoslovakia, Bonneka's country. And the people desperately wanted to help us. Again, I felt overcome by a surge of joy. Though Kay equally felt the surprise, she still didn't seem fully convinced.

"But—" she finally muttered. I patiently waited for her to say something negative, seeing as she still had a dirty stare. "Kill us here or there, what difference does it make?"

"Kay, no!" I said disapprovingly. I finally felt a sense of hope and desperately wanted to bring some life back into Kay.

The idea of seeing my family felt closer than it had in a long time. I felt the warmth of Betty in my arms, though she would now be much bigger than how I imagined her.

Kay closed her eyes. Her slumber seemed peaceful, but I could not get myself to sleep. I finally felt what it was like to have energy again.

It had been three weeks since the Bloem family last saw or heard of Bonneka.

"Perhaps she just doesn't have enough food anymore," Kees tried to comfort his wife.

"Don't make me laugh! The poor woman was frightened away by that little wench."

Stan had overheard their conversation and came into the kitchen. His face reddened.

"Danique is not a wench. Take it back!"

Now Jochem entered the living room, interested in the fuss. "Everyone knows she screws half of Amsterdam."

"That is not true!" Stan ran towards his brother and tackled him to the floor.

Their father tried to break up the fight, though his sons were much stronger than him. Jochem pushed Stan's face to the floor and pulled his arm towards his back. Stan was helplessly trying to wriggle himself out of the position but realised that his brother had the upper hand. Finally, their father managed to pull them apart and held Stan back from punching his brother again.

Loes and Annie curiously entered the room.

"Take it back!" Stan spat out. His brother laughed.

Then Zilvertje finally spoke up. "Thanks to your girlfriend, we have less food on the table."

"She couldn't have known," Stan tried, though he knew he had made a mistake.

Loes stood by, amused by the whole affair. She had always been jealous of Danique. Stan was her favourite brother, and they had spent most of their time together when they were children. Since he had become slightly older and started getting girlfriends, he was way less attentive to his younger sister.

"I think you should break up with her," she said.

"That's what you all want, isn't it? Well, Danique makes me happier than any of you, so I won't hear any more of it!" Stan got out of his father's grip and slammed the front door behind him.

Zilvertje was slightly concerned, as she knew her son could act irrationally whenever he was angry or felt misunderstood.

"I'll go after him," Jochem said, but his mother immediately stopped him.

"Let your sister go," Zilvertje said.

Loes was prepared to step forward.

"Annie, you go bring your brother back home."

She nodded and Loes gave her sister a dirty look.

"I will not tolerate fighting in this house!" Kees raised his voice. Annie left Beppy home, knowing that it would take a long while for her to find Stan. She took a tram all the way to the centre of the city, knowing that her brother probably went to Danique's house, who lived in the south of Amsterdam.

She passed the Royal Concert Hall when she saw a utility truck and tanks passing through the street towards the south of the city. A bunch of civilians stopped walking when they noticed the vehicles.

Annie found an older man nearby and asked what was happening. "Haven't you heard, dear? They are executing members of the resistance," he said casually.

"How?" she stared at him in utter disbelief.

"The KP-Amsterdam—they have been creating a stir. This might be the fourth or fifth fusillade I'm aware of."

Annie was too embarrassed to ask further questions. She thanked the man and continued walking, this time without a clear purpose of where to go. She wondered whether a lot of people knew about this and if her family had kept this information from her. Either way, she felt ignorant and had completely forgotten what she had come here to do.

When Annie arrived back home, she saw that Stan's bike was outside again, which meant he was back home. He was inside, talking to Loes, who was holding Beppy.

"Where have you been? We thought you were going to find Stan. We've been worried sick!"

Annie wondered how long she had been gone.

"Have you heard about the fusillades?" she asked her mother.

Zilvertje didn't respond, and her father was nowhere to be seen—probably somewhere else in the house, reading his newspaper.

"I want to hear about it," Loes intervened.

"All you need to know is that auntie Bonneka is being cautious. And we need to be too. The war is not over yet and we still have Beppy to take care of," Zilvertje said.

"So, it's true! They've been executing resistance fighters! Why didn't you tell me about it?" Annie became angry and Stan ignored her.

"So, I can't see my girlfriend?" he said resentfully.

"We all have to make sacrifices—the war is not over yet." Zilvertje was losing her patience.

"Stan, you have to wait until Beppy's mother is back," Loes said. Annie's stomach was rumbling, which made her feel auntie Bonneka's absence even more. Zilvertje retreated to the kitchen where she was met with an empty pantry, seeing as no one had gone to the soup kitchen in a while.

She heard her sons quarrelling yet again about Danique, and now Loes was joining them too.

"It's all because of her!" Stan pointed at Beppy. Annie joined the argument—defensive of Beppy.

Zilvertje grabbed a large pot and started filling it with water. Her kids were still arguing, and it seemed to become louder and louder, until she continually hit a metal spoon against the big pot and shouted, "Enough!" Finally, there was silence. The sounds had been so loud that even Kees had come downstairs.

Zilvertje's eyes welled up. "What happened?" her husband asked, but she ignored him and finally lost her temper.

"You ungrateful children! From now on, I don't want to hear a word from any of you unless I ask you something. Tomorrow, everyone will be going to work. After work, each of you will be queuing at the soup kitchens. Annie, you will stay at home to take care of your little sister. And listen to my words. Beppy is a little sister to each of you! I will not hear otherwise, or you will feel the back of this spoon, and I can assure you it won't be pleasant. If anyone even thinks about raising their voice or fist—you will spend the next month sleeping on the floor. Do you understand?"

All her children nodded obediently.

"Now, if you will excuse me, I shall be going on a walk to clear my mind. By the time I am back, I expect to see food on the table," Zilvertje grabbed her coat and left the house.

———————————

Upon arrival at the new work camp, I had a weird déjà vu when seeing the similar low, elongated stone buildings. They were all symmetrically placed, one behind the other, and the whole camp was surrounded by a high wall, edged with barbed wire. The barracks were similar to those we had seen before—with three-levelled wooden bunkbeds that were heavily overcrowded. This time, it was even worse. We had arrived late in the night, which meant the bunk beds were already full. Kay and I still had our blankets, so we wrapped them around us and lay on the floor next to one another.

"I can't work tomorrow," Kay whispered. "If I work, I'll die."

I remembered how it had started with Feline. She started getting irritable and losing hope, until she slowly but surely accepted the faith that they had given her. Death. I couldn't let the same thing happen to Kay.

The night had been too short, and we were woken up for a quick breakfast. "Hanna!"

An endearing voice called my name. It was one I recognised. I assumed I had misheard it, or that this person was referring to someone else.

"Hanna, it's me!" she called again, though this time it was nearer to me and I could clearly hear its familiarity. I looked around. We were being called to stand in a line, a mass of women.

Throughout the day, I kept thinking about the voice. Was I becoming delusional?

We were standing in a line to receive our watery brew they called "coffee," similar to the one we used to have at the previous camp. Only this time, they hadn't given us bowls, which meant we weren't able to have breakfast. That was always the rule—no bowl, no food.

"We should steal one," Kay said.

"And take away someone else's food? No way!"

She was disappointed by my lack of cruelty. Just like Feline had been. It seemed to be a pattern, though I didn't want things to end with Kay like they had with Feline. I had abandoned her, thinking that her fed up mood and tension would be contagious.

Without breakfast, we marched towards a workshop barrack. A female guard instructed that we should start working and finish everything before twelve or we would not receive any lunch. We hadn't had any food since our arrival anyway.

I looked at the pile of clothes in front of me. There were soldier uniforms lying there. I picked one up and observed the coat, trying to find a rip or tear. Apart from it being bloody and dirty and the missing buttons, there was nothing. The uniform was perfectly intact.

What did they want me to do here? So, I grabbed another uniform instead—same thing. I wondered whether my eyesight had deteriorated. For countless hours, I pretended to observe the uniforms and threw them from one pile to the other, wondering whether Kay was doing the same thing. I tried to look out, see what the other girls were doing. They seemed to be sorting the uniforms, ripping some pieces off. None of them spoke any Dutch, German, or even English. After a while, one of the women next to me grabbed my arm. She was wearing a grey headscarf, a few strands of dark brown fizzy curls peeking out of it. She grabbed one of the uniforms and pointed at its insigne.

"*Suvjétik,*" she whispered.

I shook my head. "What?"

She repeated the word. My mind was too tired to think, so I pretended to understand and thanked her with a smile and nod.

Without bowls, Kay and I weren't able to get any of the soup they were giving out. We sat on the wet, muddy floor. My stomach didn't rumble anymore. It had passed the point of feeling hunger. Now it was just cramps and pains. In the distance, I could see the woman with the grey headscarf. She approached us and sat next to me. The woman did have a bowl with food and held it close to her and away from us. I desperately wanted to steal her food. She put her other hand in her pocket and carefully took something out of it. She had a big loaf of black bread. She put it on my lap. Kay's eyes lit up, and I ripped the bread and gave her the other half.

I put my hand on my heart.

"Hanna," I said to the women.

She looked surprised.

"Anna," she said.

"Yes, I'm Hanna. And you?"

"Anna," she repeated.

I pointed at her and shook my head.

"No, I'm Hanna. What is *your* name?" I asked again.

She pointed at herself and said "Anna" again. We almost shared a name.

Kay introduced herself too.

We thanked her again for the bread and slowly ate it in silence. If there was one thing we had learned from being at Auschwitz, it was that one should never gulp their food, especially not if it was the first thing they had eaten in days.

I finished the last piece and enjoyed the feeling of the wheat on my tongue. It had been such a long time since I had properly eaten— it was a moment I had to savour for as long as I could.

Anna had finished her bowl and was staring into the distance. There were so many things I wanted to ask her. Where she was from, whether she had any family, how old she was, why she was here. Unlike us, the woman didn't wear a yellow star. Instead, she had a red triangle on her sleeve.

I pointed out the triangle, asking what it meant.

"*Déportés politique*," she said.

I finally understood where her accent was from.

"*Français*," I spoke triumphantly.

"*Française*," Anna corrected.

There were shouts and gunshots. We had to go back to work immediately. I hoped to be able to resume my conversation with Anna soon.

That evening, Kay and I managed to find ourselves some spaces in the bunkbeds. We had to lay on our left side and were sandwiched in between the others, but at least we got a place to sleep. We hadn't been able to go to the bathroom since our arrival—besides, there was a huge pile of dead corpses in front of it. Some women couldn't bear not being able to shower, so they would power through and pass the corridor of bodies who were rotting and had been there for days. I could not even look at them, let alone pass through them.

"You seemed to get on well with your namesake," Kay sounded a little jealous.

"She's called Anna."

"No, Hanna, for sure. The French don't pronounce their *H*s." Some girls shushed us, so I tried to close my eyes and fall asleep.

———————

We had only been at the new camp, which we now found out was called Ravensbrück, for a couple of weeks. There were rumours that we would have to walk again. I could not endure another march through hundreds of miles of cold with no rest. My body was aching more than before. My stomach was continuously overwhelmed by nausea and abdominal cramps. I hoped it wasn't because of many months of physical experiments.

Kay and I had been able to cling onto one another. She helped me walk and keep myself composed, helped me pretend I was healthy enough not to be sent to the gas chambers.

———————

One morning, before the others woke up, my hunger became unbearable. I sat upright but tried to be as quiet as I could. Kay's eyes slowly opened, and I shushed that she should go back to bed. I saw Anna sleeping in a bunk bed, only a few feet away. Her bowl was on the floor, hidden in between her torn shoes. I tiptoed slowly. The women were exhausted, but they were so agitated that even a fly could wake them up. I crawled onto the floor to quietly grab it. Still, I couldn't allow my hands to actually take it. Holding the bowl, I could already taste the broth on the tip of my tongue, its warmth covering the roof of my mouth. All I longed for was to finally indulge in a breakfast meal, so I hid the bowl under my shirt.

The girl next to Anna also had a bowl, which she was holding onto in her sleep. I wanted to steal it for Kay, not only so she would finally have some food, but also because I didn't want to share my bowl.

The girl was straining her face—it looked like she was having a nightmare. *And she was*, I thought. I took a deep breath in and slowly wrapped my fingers around the bowls handle. She didn't wake up or even flinch. It was almost too easy to take her bowl, and I had an immense feeling of guilt wash over me.

"You stole them?"

Kay was both shocked and thrilled to finally have a bowl with food.

"You see that girl?" Kay asked.

"Who?"

Kay pointed at someone.

"Her name's Maria. She came up to me yesterday, said she knows you."

My mind was still disorientated.

"She speaks Dutch."

I tried to remember why that name was so familiar. In Amsterdam, I knew quite a few women called Maria, though no one who would be here.

"Pretty girl, think she might be Spanish."

An image appeared in front of me. I recalled my moments in Westerbork with a certain Maria. I could even imagine her walking in the distance. The stature approached me. I blinked a couple of times to make sure I wasn't hallucinating.

The girl was real, and she immediately hugged me. She was in tears.

"I have been trying to find you!" It was clearly Maria's rusty voice. I tried to compose myself, make sure she could not see how weak I was.

I tried to hug her back.

"How strange the world is." She had a wide smile and was still as charming as I remembered her to be.

"Hanna saved my life," Maria told Kay.

I tried to open my mouth, but no sounds came out. I was too stunned to think of anything to say.

"Thanks to you, I stayed in Westerbork until September. *Sometimes our safety is more important than our dignity*—that's what you told me! It's what helped me stay on the down-low."

I tried to speak but could not bring myself to say a word. My throat hurt.

"Have you lost your tongue?"

Maria was also still as sarcastic as I remembered her to be.

My eyes opened abruptly. I was in bed, shoved in between two women. Kay was behind me, and my heavy breathing had woken her up. My throat still hurt a lot. I tried to recall the moment with Maria, but only remembered it as a foggy memory or a faraway dream.

"Where is Maria?"

Kay laughed. "Who?"

My expression was sincere. "Maria, the girl I met at Westerbork? I spoke to her earlier today!"

"We didn't see any woman called Maria . . ."

My face turned pale. I was losing my mind.

––––––––––––

Bonneka had one hand in her pockets, firmly holding onto a sealed envelope. In the other, she was carrying a bag. She paced through the streets of Amsterdam.

It had been a couple of months since she been to visit one of the households where someone was in hiding. Since that incident with the Bloem family, Nol had told her to keep on the down-low. It was too dangerous. Every day, she had wanted to go back to them, bring them food, and see if Beppy was alright. Nevertheless, she understood Nol's worries and made sure to stay away from the family.

It was still very cold and windy, though the hunger was luckily diminishing. Bonneka listened to the radio to hear about the slow but steady political improvements which could help defeat the Germans. The hunger had lasted way too long, which was why Bonneka was thrilled to hear of the Swedish and Swiss governments helping the country. These international aids would help save the Netherlands.

On her walk, she contemplated whether she would try to visit the Bloem's household—just to make sure they received enough of the Swedish bread that was being handed out to civilians.

Finally, Bonneka approached a three-story row house. She left the bag in front of the door, took the letter out of her pocket, and shoved it through the door's letterbox flap. She knocked but made sure to quickly leave before anyone opened.

Moor rushed to her front door. She wondered who would be visiting their house on a Sunday morning. No one was there, though she found a bag on the doorstep and a couple of letters on the doormat. One of them was addressed to Ab, which surprised her.

"Who is it?" her partner, Hansje, shouted from the kitchen. The house smelt of French toast. Not only was it the first time in a while that they had leftover bread, but today was also Ab's birthday. So, the women wanted to make sure he would have a pleasant day.

"There's a letter. For Ab!"

Moor opened the bag.

"And *boterkoek*," she said, smelling the delicious butter-filled treat. "What are you waiting for then? Give it to him!" Moor ran upstairs and woke him up. Ab and a few others had been staying in their attic. But Jews weren't the only thing these two women were hiding.

"Come on, birthday boy." She threw the letter on his lap. "Get up! There's a royal breakfast for all of you this morning."

Ab stared at the letter in front of him. Could it be from his sister? He hadn't heard anything from her since they had last seen each other. He still thought about her every single day. The Gestapo had found out where she and Nico were in hiding, and he was constantly worried of what might happen to them. Luckily, his friend, Louis, had managed to keep Ab calm. Besides, Betty was still safe, and he knew his sister. She was a courageous woman and would stand her ground. That, he felt sure of.

Ab opened the letter.

> March 4, 1945
> Dear Ab,
> We wish you much joy and a happy birthday, from the both of us. May you have a nice day. We hope that you will relish our baked treat. Anyhow, things have been looking up, and we believe that it might even be so that we could have a drink together by the end of this month. Kind regards from both of us,
> Nol & Bonneka

"Ab, get that birthday smirk off your face. You haven't even read the poem I wrote you," Louis joked.

A peculiar birthday, it certainly was, and Ab knew how lucky he was to enjoy it with Hansje, Moor, Louis, and the others in hiding. And he felt especially grateful for Bonneka and Nol's kind message.

The women brought the butter cake upstairs, along with a single lit candle.

"Goddammit, don't make me partake in that ridiculous tradition," Ab smirked.

"Make a wish!" Hansje insisted.

He caved and blew out the candle. Though feeling slightly ridiculous, he decided to make a single wish—for his sister to be safe.

"What did you wish for?" Louis asked.

"Don't tell us or it won't come true!"

They all took a piece of the butter cake and tucked into the sweet and richly tender pastry.

"To Hanna and Nico," Ab said, "that you may meet them soon!"

SPRING, 1945

WE HAD ARRIVED at a new camp yet again. Only, this time, it didn't look like we were here to work through the daily monotonous, yet unpredictable routine. Death had always been around the corner, lurking through just one gunshot, beating, or standing in the wrong line. Now it was too close. And its name was Neustadt-Glewe.

The officers forcefully led us through the camp, all the way to a hangar in its centre. In that hangar, I stared death in its eyes. The hall was full of sick people; there was lots of diarrhea everywhere. Definitely not a hospital, as it seemed on the outside.

I recognised the same people, the ones I had been at Auschwitz with. It felt ironic to see all of them, even sicker and thinner now than they had been before. We had survived that place, only to arrive in Germany and be even worse off.

Kay held my hand tightly. We hadn't let go since leaving Ravensbrück. She tried to warm my hand, though it wasn't just my hand that was cold. Regardless of the balmy weather and strong sunlight, my body still ached as though the winter hadn't ended.

"The sick ones to the left!" An officer shouted. I had been shivering and feeling unwell for quite some time now, so I moved to the left side.

Kay grabbed my arm. "You know what they do with ill people."

She was right. So, I decided to stand still and wait. One of the officers saw that I was barely able to keep my head up, and he approached me. "Sick ones to the left!" he repeated. There was no way I could pretend anymore, so I obeyed and walked in line with all the others who were headed for the camp's "hospital."

The place was filthy and full of naked bodies and rotting corpses. There were rats eating the insides of those laying on the floor. I looked away and had to throw up. The officers laughed.

"On that bed," one of them pointed at a dirty mattress barely held up by a rusty metal frame. There was another woman laying on it, her body black and blue. I tried to keep myself up and say that I was fine, though I was only fooling myself. Finally, I lay down next to the woman. She didn't even notice me. The space was so small that I had to lay on my side. My eyelids became heavy, and I could finally have some rest.

A nurse woke me up.

She had a few documents with her and asked for my name and checked the number that was tattooed on my arm: 63228.

"What are you going to do with this?"

She didn't understand what I was saying; my head was too dizzy to be able to properly articulate. Then the nurse took my temperature, showed me my file, and asked whether it was all spelled correctly. There were a few words I couldn't read, though I understood one of them clearly.

It said *Typhus*.

I pointed at the word and shook my head.

"Two weeks, then you're out."

It didn't feel like enough time to heal. And besides, it seemed as though the prisoners at the hospital were getting more ill rather than better. Even though I wasn't sure of what was happening outside the hospital barrack, it must've been better than being stuck inside this place. If I could've gotten up, then I would have walked straight out of there. But my body didn't allow me that luxury. After a couple of days, I realised that the woman next to me wasn't breathing anymore. I tried to call for one of the nurses, but there was no one around. I tried to speak to the woman. No response.

I grabbed her wrist, and there was no heartbeat. So, I checked her neck; then I rested my hand on her chest. This woman was clearly dead. I pushed her off the bed. Her lifeless body fell with a load thud. I was ashamed, though no one had even noticed. The spot where she had lain was wet with blood, mud, and urine. Still, I decided to roll over. I could finally fully stretch my body on the dirty mattress.

I recognised a voice in the distance and realised it was Kay. She had come to visit me.

"Is the war over?" I whispered.

Even though I was happy to see her, I couldn't move to hug her. And even if I could, I wanted to make sure not to infect her. I barely knew anything about the disease, only that it was probably contagious, which we had realised back in Auschwitz when people in overfull barracks would get infected with it and sent to the gas chambers.

"Are they going to kill me?" I asked.

Kay looked around the room.

"Look at this place, and they call this a hospital!" She grabbed my arm.

I immediately got out of her grip and said, "I have typhus; it's contagious."

She told me to trust her. So, I did.

"I have to be here for two weeks."

"And it has been," Kay said.

I was shocked. Had I been here for so long? They had barely been treating my wounds and infections. When I leaned to my left, I could see that the nurse was there too. She was signing me out.

"But I'm not better," I groaned, grabbing the nurse's apron and pulling it towards me.

"You can talk. You're better," she pushed me back.

Kay helped me walk, and we left the hospital barrack. Some guards, who had been standing outside, yelled at us to get back to our barrack. One of them spat at me, and I licked my teeth. It reminded me of a German soldier in Amsterdam, who had made that same hocking noise before spitting on the floor and calling me *horse teeth*.

We arrived at a smaller wooden barrack, just like the one I saw on my arrival at Auschwitz back in September, 1943. Only, this time, everything was different.

I thought I would never miss that place, though now I craved to go back there. At least there we had a routine. The barracks were always grim, but never as bad as the ones in Neustadt. At Auschwitz, we knew when we'd receive food, and if we made sure to obey and stayed strong enough to work hard, then we wouldn't starve or die. This place scared me. The fact that there was no work scared me. The ill and weak prisoners scared me—wandering around like zombies waiting to enter their grave. I had a rash on my chest that didn't seem to go away. From what we had heard, the camp used to be a place where the prisoners worked on the production of aeroplanes in the hangar. But that wasn't happening anymore—nothing was.

———

One night, I was on the floor, noticing an officer staring at me intensely. He didn't look like the other officers. He had a gentler glare, though I was doubting myself and afraid that the man wasn't actually showing me kindness. I might have been imagining it. Or worse, the man might have not even been there at all.

The next morning, he was gone. I was slightly disappointed to not see him when I woke up. A few hours later, he was back. He looked at me again, and this time, he gave a slight smile. A look of reassurance. I forced myself to stand up and approached him, hoping that he would have some food or water.

He took my arm, startling me. Without saying a word, he took me outside. I couldn't let out any words. There were only two things running through my mind—either he would beat me or rape me. I hoped it would be the second one, for I could not endure another beating and was afraid it might kill me.

In Auschwitz and Birkenau, there had been brothels. I would see the officers entering them all the time, and whenever they got out, their moods would be slightly better, less aggressive, only for a little while.

I followed him to the back of the barrack, closer to an empty field with no one in sight. There was no part of my body that managed to resist him, so I merely obeyed. He sat me down on the floor.

"Stay," he said in German. He had a deep voice with a soothing quality. A couple of minutes later, he came back with water, bread, and a raw onion. "For you."

I smelt it, assuming one of these would be poisonous, though I was too thirsty and hungry to resist the temptation.

"Good girl," he said as I started drinking from the cup.

It didn't take me long to finish.

"Slow down!"

He looked me up and down.

"Do you speak German?"

"*Ein bisschen. Ich verstehe dich.*"

I understand you, I replied. This time, I took a bite of the onion. In the past, I wouldn't have been able to stand the strong flavour of the raw root vegetable, but now, it tasted like an aromatic and delicious treat. Also slightly tear-inducing. The man could see the tears rolling down my face, and I hoped that he wouldn't think they were sentimental. It was a thing I hadn't done in a long while, cry—something my father always used to frown upon, claiming I'm an overly emotional girl.

The officer wiped my tears, which now actually made me feel slightly sentimental.

"Why are you doing this?"

No one had been kind to me in so long, I had forgotten what it felt like.

Especially coming from a man in a uniform.

"You have the power of a fighter. I can see it." My gaze shifted towards his insigne.

"I'm no SS'er," he said with disgust. "Just a *Wehrmacht* officer in an SS-uniform."

"*Wehrmacht*?" I felt foolish for asking.

"Not all Germans are monsters."

Although his statement made sense, it was something I had completely forgotten. In the camps, there had been a very clear distinction between who was good and who was bad. The officers were definitely the bad ones. It almost shook me to hear this man speak with such care. I was waiting for the catch.

"May I?" he asked, looking at my hand. I nodded. He carefully took my wrist, resting it in his hand. He tutted disapprovingly.

"You need more food."

Then he put my palm down, and his fingers went over my knuckles. I thought he would comment on the bruises and cuts.

"A piano player?" he asked.

"How do you know?"

"Only those who play have such articulate fingers."

He put my hand back down and took something out of his pocket. I was astonished and had to blink a few times to make sure my mind wasn't playing tricks on me.

"For emergencies."

He handed me half a bar of chocolate, something which I hadn't seen in almost two years. Even though I desperately wanted to take a bite, I held myself together.

"How can I ever thank you?" I asked.

"By staying alive. Freedom is among you, closer than ever before. Just remember me when that time comes."

"Did you sleep with him?" Kay asked with disbelief.

I shushed her. "Of course not!"

We sat in the corner of the room, facing the wall and making sure no one could see what we were up to. I carefully broke two tiny pieces of the chocolate bar and gave one to Kay We looked around us and simultaneously put the pieces in our mouths. The bittersweet flavour enriched my tongue. I pushed it against the roof of my mouth and felt an intense momentary joy. I wasn't only tasting the indulgent aroma, but also re-experiencing the unexpected kindness. The combination of both sensations gave me such delight.

The chocolate reminded me of my mother, Johanna. She came from a very rich family; they used to own orange plantations in Spain. When I was eight years old, almost a decade before my family had lost their fortune, we went to visit the plantations. We went in winter, during the mid-season harvest period. On a chilly evening, my parents, Ab, and I were invited to the house of a Spanish couple, whom my parents had become acquainted with. Ab and I joked that mother and the man of the house must have had a relationship of some sort when they were younger. Even though we were still kids, our joking around must have had some truth in it. That evening, we were greeted with a dinner table full of Sephardic dishes. After a very filling meal, my little brother and I left the table to go play outside. We loved the wide-open air, even when the weather was cold and the sky dark.

After an hour, mother called us back inside. We had been running around, so we didn't realise how cold our hands and feet were.

Whilst the grown-ups were indulging in red wine, the lady of the house called us into the kitchen. Tita was her name.

She was stirring into a large pot on top of the stove.

"I have a surprise for you two," she said.

Tita poured us two cups of liquid from inside the pot.

"It's cacao powder with milk, sugar, spices, and my secret ingredient, orange flower water."

I wondered why she revealed to us her secret ingredient, as I imagined it was something one should keep to themselves. Regardless, the combination of the citrusy orange with the dark taste of the cacao was a flavour which had stayed with me for many years.

Whilst biting the piece of chocolate, which had already half melted in my mouth, I remembered the flavour of that hot chocolate. It was as if I could sense the aroma of an orange as the chocolate's aftertaste.

It briefly made me forget where I was. I put the rest of the bar inside my pocket. There were four squares left. Two for me and two for Kay. But now my sweet tooth was satisfied, and I decided to keep the rest for when we both really needed it, which I imagined would be soon enough.

Kay put her hand on my shoulder and whispered, "I want to go back to Auschwitz."

I never thought this was something I would ever say, but I answered, "Me too."

It had been months since I last saw Aron. He wasn't in Neustadt with us, or at least I hadn't seen him. Part of me hoped I would find him here at some point, though I did not want him to see me like this, and I imagined he wouldn't want me to experience the state he'd be in either. And another part hoped that he was free. If the rumours were true, then by now, the Soviets should have liberated the place, and Aron should be free. Unless the SS managed to evacuate the whole camp. Or worse.

Thoughts about Aron immediately brought me back to Nico.

Almost as if Aron was just a distraction. Nico was the one I really missed, and the one I knew I'd never see again.

I sat on my knees and prayed. As a woman, I normally wouldn't be allowed to say Kadish, a prayer in honour of the deceased. But the rules didn't matter, and so I whispered it softly. A couple of people around me could hear and started whispering with me, slightly louder. The whispering led into song, and before we knew it, everyone was singing. Uncontrolled and out of tune, but loudly, nonetheless. Kay stared at me in awe.

It brought a very short-lived sense of community, which we hadn't felt since Birkenau. "You managed to get a bar of chocolate and make the whole barrack sing in less than a day," Kay said, baffled.

My vision became hazy, and I vaguely heard the loud thud with which I fell to the ground. The only thing I could see was the darkness behind my eyelids, and the last thing I heard was Kay shouting my name.

———————

Annie took Beppy for a walk through the city. They passed by Artis, the zoo, which had had a lot of problems during the famine.

"It must be so difficult to feed all those large animals," Annie remarked.

"Ducks!" Beppy answered proudly.

"No, not ducks. Those are the small animals that we feed in the park. After the war, I'll take you to the zoo. We can see the elephants, the monkeys . . ."

Beppy repeated the words with delight. "They also have a very nice petting zoo."

Annie kept to herself that a lot of the farm animals had been stolen the previous winter by hungry families.

When they arrived home, Annie sat the little girl down, though she constantly wanted to get up and walk around.

"You can't stay still, can you?" she laughed.

Beppy was confidently running around and speaking half-sentences about elephants and monkeys.

"And she can't shut up either." Jochem got out of the bathroom and put on his coat and hat. "Where are you going?"

"Haven't you heard the news? Arnhem just got liberated by British troops. We're one step closer to being free from those pigs!"

Beppy proudly repeated, "Pigs!"

Jochem closed the door behind him. He was probably going to celebrate with his workmates and drink a couple of beers. Every day, they seemed to be a step closer to liberation, and this made Annie happy as well as worried. She really wanted Beppy to meet her own mother, but she had a slight fear that the woman would take Beppy away from them forever. She knew that this was a silly thought, but it still worried her. The little girl felt more like a sister to her than any of her actual siblings. Annie couldn't imagine spending her days without Beppy by her side.

"Mama," the little girl babbled.

She held out her arms, asking Annie to pick her up. It was as though she was reading Annie's mind.

"Yes, you will meet her soon."

She kissed Beppy's forehead—yawning and squinting her eyes.

Annie began to sing her little sister's favourite lullaby:

"Sleep Beppy, sleep,
Outside, there is a sheep.
A sheep with little white feet,
Who drinks its milk so sweet.
Sleep Beppy, sleep,
Outside, there is a sheep."

The little girl murmured the lyrics with her. A tear rolled over

Annie's cheek as she stared at the girl falling asleep in her arms. She was a lot heavier now than when she first arrived at the house, and a lot louder, too.

"You will meet your mama soon," Annie whispered once more before putting Beppy in her crib and letting her fall asleep.

Kay was trying to feed me some grass she had picked outside. My lips were sealed together.

"You have to eat!" Kay insisted.

Many people had been eating grass or mud, but that was where I drew the line.

"I would rather starve."

My voice was hoarse, and whenever I opened my mouth to speak, Kay tried to shove the grass in it.

"You already are! *Safety over dignity.* Isn't that what you always say?" I shook my head. She threw the grass on the floor, then she placed her hand on my forehead and wiped away the sweat.

"You're still boiling."

I had been bedbound for a week. Not that it mattered—we had no responsibilities nor any routine, for that matter. And I wasn't the only one who couldn't lift a foot. The whole barrack was full of corpses—or people in line to become one. Kay was feeling ill, too, though she still had the force to walk, whereas I could barely sit up.

She began unbuttoning my shirt.

"Is the rash gone?" I asked quietly. Speaking was hard and painful, though Kay understood what I said. She pulled the shirt off my shoulder, then she rolled up my sleeves, without answering my question. She moved to my legs and started rolling my trousers up too.

"Kay?"

Her silence worried me.

"I'm not a child. Tell me what's going on."

"It's everywhere," she shrieked.

"Get away from me," I tried to shout. "It's contagious."

Every single word I wanted to say took me a lot of effort to express. Kay stood up and took a step back, though she seemed too weak to leave the barrack. I had seen other prisoners with the same rash.

I wanted to tell Kay to find the nice officer who had given me the chocolate. But it felt too foolish to put into words. What could he do about it? I didn't even know the man's name, and he didn't know mine. And, besides, most of the officers had already left us to die. For one mere second, I felt utterly hopeless. I couldn't think straight, let alone know how to keep myself alive. It had all lasted for too long.

I could hear a few whispers. Kay was speaking to someone else, but I couldn't keep my eyes open to see who it was.

Some of the whispers mentioned typhus. My body was losing the fight.

Betty came into my mind. The day I had given birth to her, she had been such a small baby, wrapped inside a cream-coloured blanket. I missed her so, and Nico too. I wanted him to be alive and well. I was longing for someone to care for and for someone who would take care of me. Kay tried, though an injured rat and a wounded pigeon can only take care of one another for so long.

Uniformed men entered the barrack covering their mouths and noses.

I recognised their uniforms. They were similar to the bloody ones I had seen at Ravensbrück, when we had to sort them. And then it dawned on me. When Anna, the French woman, had said, "*Suvjétik*," she actually meant *Soviet*. Their uniforms had the same insigne.

These men weren't Germans—they were Russians. Some people stood up; others couldn't. I was one of the ones who couldn't. Those who were able to cheered, tears in their eyes. Kay held my hand. The soldiers came closer to the women in the barrack; instead of helping them get up, they forced themselves onto them. No one understood what was happening. The group of soldiers spread out across the barrack and grabbed the women's bony legs and teared their trousers apart. Most women weighed less than seventy pounds, but that didn't seem to matter to them. My vision was blurry, though I heard the screams of the women whilst the soldiers began unbuttoning their trousers and raping them. Kay tried to duck and hide herself. I couldn't move. There were screams, thrusts, and groans. A soldier came closer and looked at me. The fact that I was unable to get up made me an easy target. Then he noticed Kay, crouching down on the floor. He took her wrist and pulled her up. I forced myself to make a sound. Kay was screaming whilst the soldier turned her around and took down her trousers. I saw the terror in her eyes.

"Typhus!" I was out of breath, though at least I could produce a single sound. The soldier took a step back, still holding Kay in his grip. I pointed my quivering finger at Kay and tried to repeat, "Typh—"

This time, the soldier took a step back, and one of his friends, who was holding onto another girl, pulled a face of disgust. They spoke in Russian, and I vaguely heard them say the word "typh" a few times. He still had Kay in his grip, so I had to try something else. Eventually, I ripped my shirt open to reveal my chest—covered in a repulsive rash. When the soldier saw my skin, he immediately let go of Kay, and she fell onto the ground. He repulsively moved away and wiped his hands on his trousers. She got back up and held onto me. Our shaking bodies were trying to remain as still as possible. The raping seemed to last for hours, as though each soldier wanted to try as many girls as he could.

———————

Nol threw his newspaper on Bonneka's empty plate. She had prepared an elaborate breakfast to celebrate the good news.

"Nazi Germany collapses ingloriously!" she read out loud. "We've got those bastards!"

"Reports from Switzerland and Sweden say that Hitler might be dead!"

"The downfall of the third *reich*," he sang in glory.

Amsterdam was still under German occupation, though they all knew that capitulation was only a matter of days or even hours.

Nol took a slice of bread and smeared it with margarine and some fresh cheese. Bonneka was too excited to eat. She had prepared herself a slice of bread with homemade jam and margarine, but only took a small bite.

She looked up at Nol. "I hope they come home soon."

He knew what she meant. Most of the families they helped go into hiding were still safely out of sight. But Nico and Hansje hadn't been this lucky.

"They have been away for almost three years. I'm sure they're counting the days until they can be home again."

Her gut was filled with worry. She tried to shake off the nagging feeling and enjoy her breakfast. It would be a matter of days until Hanna and Nico would be able to come home and reunite with their daughter. Bonneka was imagining how it would be. She would prepare a dinner for all of them, including Ab, and they would toast to a good end of the war. That thought made her smile.

"Stay with us, Madam." A nurse was standing over me, trying to lift my back so I could slightly lean forward. She put a pill in my mouth and gave me a cup with water to wash it down. They had already given me micro-doses of food, but nothing seemed to stay in my body for long. I was losing a lot of liquid.

The nurse explained where I was. "There is no need to be afraid anymore. You are in a school which is set up as an emergency hospital. And we won't rest until you get better."

My eyes were dreary, and I could barely feel my bones. The nurse had a kind voice, though it brought me back to the moments on the medical table in Birkenau. There too, nurses had been standing over me, giving me pills and injections and forcing me into certain positions. And the same thing had happened in the hospital barrack at Neustadt-Glewe. Only, there, they had left me to die. This time, I had to remind myself that it wasn't destructive, though my mind couldn't shake off the alarming feeling. Kay was next to me, speaking to the nurse. She hadn't left my side for a single second.

"You've been so brave," she said.

I tried to wriggle my toes and fingers but couldn't feel any movement. I stared at the ceiling, trying to put my focus onto a single point. A cloudiness appeared from my eyes, and I felt a frustration as my vision became worse and worse. I could no longer control any part of my body. There were so many women around me, crying out and thanking the nurses. I still vaguely heard their voices, as though they came from a far-away distance. Unlike these strong women, I could not cry or thank or form a single sentence, for that matter. My voice was leaving me, but I still forced myself to utter something to Kay.

"Thank you."

She cried.

My limbs and torso were already lifeless. Only my face was still awake for a single second, though my vision was blurred.

"Stay with me!"

Kay's strong voice sounded like one from a far-away distance, too. There was just a single image in front of my closed eyes. It was one of Betty—only, she wasn't a baby, but a child. She was wearing a school uniform and kissing her uncle Ab goodbye before putting on her backpack and leaving for school. Her skin was that of coffee, darker than the other girls, and her hair was almost pitch-black. She had these deep pearly eyes that brightened in the cold Dutch winter sun. I saw the girl hopping on the playground surrounded by a group of other girls and boys. People respected her. Outspoken like her uncle, clever like her father, and brave like her mother. Nico and

I were standing in front of this girl on the playground. Almost too mature for her age, but still full of playfulness. She couldn't see us. She was too focused on the games on the school playground. Nico held my hand. I loved the smell of his gelled-back hair and the hint of eau de Cologne, the same that he wore on our wedding day.

The touch of his cold hand didn't bother me. There was an immense comfort in his soft touch. He squeezed my hand as we watched Betty run across the stone tiles on the playground. Now she was not a child anymore, but a teenager. Standing outside the school, smoking a cigarette with her best friend. They were reading their end of term report cards, and Betty didn't look all too happy. She had failed quite a few of her classes and would have to retake the year if she didn't improve her grades. Nico was disapprovingly shaking his head, and I put my head on his shoulder. "Let her be. School isn't the most important thing in this world, you know that."

He turned around to notice the glimmer of hope in my eyes and nodded. "You're right."

Next thing we knew, Betty was all grown up, wearing a wedding dress. Nineteen years of age, she was standing outside the Portuguese synagogue in Amsterdam with her future husband. Still, she couldn't see us, even though we were standing there. Her beautiful smile resembled mine. Nico and I were full of pride.

I found myself lying in that hospital bed and knew it was too late. I was exhausted. My body had fought for so long, only to give in to its indolent surrender. And now, my mind was ready to go, too. It was time to finally accept. I murmured one last prayer for Betty until I fell asleep, knowing and embracing that I would have my last breath in freedom.

SPRING, 2015

IN THE EARLY MORNING, they left Amsterdam. Betty sat in the passenger seat. Her son was driving. Her two daughters were sitting in the back. They had been driving for almost six hours and finally arrived at their destination.

Immediately, they parked the car in front of the cemetery and walked towards an empty field, a mass grave. The sky was free of clouds, and the sun shone upon their faces. In front of the field, there was a simple square monument, surrounded by nothing but large patches of grass, bushes, and trees. Even though the concentration camp had completely vanished, there was still a strange feeling surrounding the area. Betty's son took a tiny piece of paper out of his pocket—a prayer, Yizkor. The two sisters looked up at their little brother, who was now a middle-aged man. He unexpectedly murmured the prayer, and the three women looked down at the ground in silence.

That quietness continued, even when they left the monument to walk towards the town. Seventy years ago, the town's inhabitants had seen all the bodies of the deceased being dragged through the streets. Now, the place was so peaceful and quiet. A sweet Saturday afternoon.

"Strange, isn't it," one of her daughters said on the way to their hotel. Once they arrived there, the four of them were treated like guests of honour. They entered a lounge with tables full of coffee, tea, and treats. The mayor of the town gave a speech, and most people present were surrounding the now seventy-three year-old Betty. An extrovert lady who could make a whole room laugh and engage in her stories—though Betty felt she needed something else. She took her three children aside and asked if they could leave the lounge to go for dinner. Just the four of them. They gladly accepted and spent the evening full of innocent laughter, good food, cheers, and wine.

Betty raised her glass. "I also want to make a toast to my surrogate mum." To this day, Annie was still Betty's special, go-to person, the one who knew her best. And so, they raised their glasses.

The next morning, they were silent again. On this day, seventy years ago, Hanna had passed away, in a nearby school which had been turned into an emergency hospital. The mass grave monument was still the same. Betty, who rarely cried, finally let out all the tears she had been holding onto for all those years. The tears for her mother, Hanna, who had never cried at Auschwitz. After the war, Betty had been raised by her uncle Ab and his wife Jetty. Whenever Betty would cry, her uncle always said, "You remind me of your mother." So, the tears were one of the simple things that made her feel closer to Hanna. Now it was Betty's turn to say a prayer. As a woman, she normally wouldn't be allowed to say Kadish, a prayer in honour of the deceased. But the rules didn't matter, and so she whispered it softly. Her tears hadn't fully dried, yet her stance and intentions were so firm. A strong vulnerability, just like her mother. When she finished saying the prayer, they all stared at the mass grave for a little longer.

Betty smiled and looked at her children. She thought of her grandchildren, all eight of them. Hanna's legacy.

Betty's voice was slightly shaking when she said, "Now, seventy years later, it feels like I've finally buried my mother."

Hanna passed away on 3 May 1945, in Neustadt-Glewe; she was thirty-one years old.

Nico passed away on 20 December 1943, in Monowitz; he was thirty-two years old.

Ab passed away on 22 June 1983, in Amsterdam; he was sixty-eight years old.

Annie passed away on 7 August 2015, in Amsterdam; she was eighty-six years old. Annie's obituary mentioned her two children, along with Betty as Annie's oldest daughter.

Betty is still alive and well today.

AFTERWORD

HANNA IS MY GREAT GRANDMOTHER. It was her journey that inspired me to write this book. Hanna's blood runs through my veins; although, we never actually met. I sometimes have these intrusive thoughts when I think about what would've happened if I'd been alive in the 1940s. What if I had been Hanna?

There are a number of things that triggered and stimulated my curiosity.

My grandmother, Betty, has countless pictures of Hanna—pictures of what her life was like before the war, when she used to go on trips with her friends, when she got married to the love of her life, Nico. She also has letters that Hanna sent to her father and her brother Ab as well as passports, and so much more. There's a whole narrative to be found in these pre-war photographs and documents. Really fascinating stuff.

Every person has a story that's worth telling. It's Hanna's story that I chose to tell. She was just a woman, living her life, until a force beyond her control changed her whole path; along the way, she made brave but questionable decisions. Still, I am very aware that, without one of those decisions, I would never have been alive today.

Writing this book, therefore, seemed like the natural thing to do. After having done a fair share of external research in combination with a lot of soul searching, I managed to create a balance between her true story and how she had been living her life in my imagination. She was alive during a period in history that is reflected in so much modern-day fiction and memoirs. Yet all these stories are unique. It was never my intention to write my book about the holocaust. On the contrary, I just wanted to accumulate everything we knew about Hanna into a bigger picture, to create a true understanding of who she was and what she was about. And whilst writing, I felt privileged to be able to create a story around her face and name so that my family and I could finally get to know the person she had been.

Sadly, this story is exceptionally relevant today; there are still concentration camps in the world. Families are being separated, and innocent people are imprisoned. These camps seem to be a product of our technologically advanced society, whereby twentieth-century inventions such as barbed wire and advanced bureaucracy are used alongside barbaric medieval torture methods and violations of basic human rights. The only difference between the 1940s and today is that we do have the powerful ability to immediately see what is happening in the world. With a single click, we can learn about these atrocities and speak up.

Hanna was an incredible woman. Fierce, loyal, kind, and dedicated. Unfortunately, there are so many Hanna's out there. I only hope that their stories will be told when they're alive so that they have the chance to be saved.

Betty and her stepbrother.

Hannah and Ab.

Hanna and Nico.

Hanna in Scheveningen, 1930.

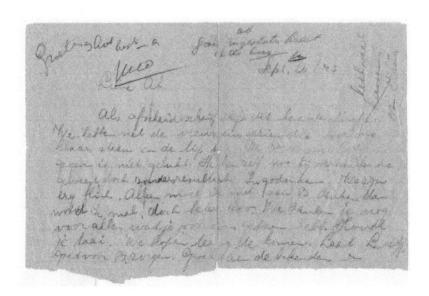

Letter to Ab from Westerbork, 1943.

CPSIA information can be obtained
at www.ICGtesting.com
Printed in the USA
LVHW041411030822
725020LV00004B/194